THE DOCKYARD DARLING

ANNIE SHIELDS

PROLOGUE

*H*e despised London.

From the opulent hotels in Mayfair to the squalid streets of the East End, where a man's life could be snuffed out for a mere tuppence, the city teetered on a razor's edge. Yet London stood proud, as those who worshipped at her filthy feet arrogantly claimed it was the greatest city in the world.

Buildings huddled together, leaning into one another like drunken sailors in a doss house. The moonlight, choked by the impenetrable fog, struggled to pierce the gloom that clung to the crumbling edifices and slithered through the damp streets. By day, the city was shrouded in a suffocating veil of smoke, the buildings scorched black from the soot-laden air. By night, it throbbed with an undercurrent of peril.

Faceless figures shuffled through the darkness, their skeletal hands outstretched in a desperate plea for alms, for food. Others huddled in darkened doorways, announcing their presence only with a cough in the blackness. The meagre light from the towering black gas lamps cast a sinister glow on the damp cobblestones.

He strode with purpose, the echo of his footsteps announcing his presence to the shadowy forms lurking in the unseen corners where the dim lights dared not venture. His eyes darted from side to side, awareness thrumming in his veins as he navigated the treacherous heart of this malevolent city.

Even at this ungodly hour, the distant clatter of hooves echoed through the murky air. Beyond the deceptive glow, dark alleyways snaked away from the grimy lanes, concealing untold threats.

He yearned for the rolling fields of home, but he had a job to do. He hiked his collar up against the biting chill. He could feel the eyes of unseen watchers tracking his every move from the shadows' depths, past the gaslights' feeble reach. Carriages rumbled past, narrowly avoiding the lifeless heaps that littered the streets. Sometimes the rag-clad bodies stirred; other times, they were carted away by the undertaker.

The stench of the docklands wafted on the breeze that wrapped around him like a treacherous lover. That's where she was said to be hiding. He pressed on, the reek of rotten fish assaulting his senses. The wind had picked up, nudging the fog back, revealing the proud masts in the faint glow of the docks. The gentle lapping of the river against the quayside whispered in his ear, a siren's call to the danger that lay ahead.

He had a mission to complete. He would see it through, and then he would return home. Back to clean air and green fields. He would find her here amongst the sailors and the traders. He knew they would turn on their own kin for a coin, like a rat chewing off its tail to escape the trap.

It shouldn't take long. She was just a girl.

OH, how he loathed London.

CHAPTER 1

*T*he second Ella Tomlinson opened her eyes, she knew that something was wrong.

"What is it, Milly?" Ella whispered to the young maid who hovered at the foot of her bed.

The candlelight danced eerily across the girl's features as Ella blinked into the gloom of her bedroom.

"Please, Miss," Milly whispered, laying a finger across her lips in a signal for Ella to lower her voice. "Mrs Green might hear and I... I'm not meant to be in here."

Ella pulled herself into a sitting position and rubbed her eyes. "What's the matter?"

"It's your father, Miss," Milly held out a house coat as she looked back at the bedroom door.

Her somnolent mind stuttered. "My father?"

"You must come quickly but do it quietly. Please, Ella, hurry."

Unsure whether it was the use of her name or the

urgency that shimmered around the girl, Ella shoved back the bed covers, icy fingers of dread sliding through her. Milly may just be a servant, but Ella had come to trust her. Perhaps it was the times that Ella hid out in the kitchen to escape from her annoying younger brother, Thomas. Perhaps it was their mutual love of literature, but their unusual friendship meant a lot to Ella. The young girl saw and heard things that had kept Ella abreast of the spiteful machinations of her stepmother for years.

"What's wrong with him?" Ella asked. The night air sent gooseflesh across her bare legs when she shoved her hands into the sleeves of her gown. The fire had long since died and not a wisp of heat remained in the room. She cinched the belt at her waist and pushed her black hair away from her face.

"I don't know, Miss. Doctor Seward is here."

Ella couldn't hide her surprise as she stared at the maid. The doctor was a regular house visitor, tending to her brother's inventory of ill health. But for him to be making a house visit in the middle of the night meant that something was very wrong indeed.

"Where are they?"

"Your father is in his study, Miss. Mrs Tomlinson sent Willie out to fetch him. She told Mrs Green that you weren't to be disturbed but I…"

Ella bit back the sigh. She should be used to the malevolent agenda of her stepmother by now. "It's fine," Ella held out a hand for the candle that Milly had lit for her. "I'll think of something. Go back to your room."

They each went their separate ways along the corridor. Ella checked that Milly was safe beyond the end of the corridor before she hurried down the narrow staircase to the floor below.

Having a bedroom in between the family level and the servant's level in the attic had often been a source of controversy between her father and her stepmother. But her father's work took him away from the home for extended periods and it meant that Clara very often got her own way in these things. Henry Tomlinson quite often took the path of less resistance when it came to his indulged younger wife though it was often Ella that bore the brunt of the direction that those paths went in. The truth was that Ella didn't mind having the floor to herself. She didn't really mind the times when Clara banished her to the bedroom for the mild infractions that her stepmother imagined. Ella had accepted long ago that her stepmother saw Ella as an inconvenience at best, and a challenge to any inheritance due to her younger brother at worst.

She passed by the door to her brother's room; it was firmly shut, and she wondered if she should check on him. Thomas was not quite fourteen but had always been a sickly child. As much as the small boy held animus towards her, she cared a great deal for him. She hesitated for just a moment before continuing along the corridor. Milly wanted her to hurry.

Ella paused at the foot of the wide staircase. Two of the wall sconces remained lit, and the shadows cast by her candle danced along the walls and across the garish-coloured floor tiles that Clara had insisted on installing to make her mark on the grand property. She cocked her ear to listen carefully. She could just about make out urgent whispering though it wasn't coming from the direction of the study, but the library. Perhaps Milly had been wrong, and her father was in a different room.

Ella made her way across the hall, her bare feet whispering across the tiles. But she stopped when she made out Clara's husky laugh. She took a breath to steady her nerves before she faced the wrath of her stepmother whom would no doubt be furious that she was out of bed. Her hand rested against the wooden door as if to open it though she paused when she made out Doctor Seward's deep voice.

"Clara, you should have waited."

Even on the other side of the door, Ella could make out her stepmother's irritated tut. "I've waited for long enough, Albert." Clara's voice was clipped with annoyance. "I can't wait any longer, so I decided to take things into my own hands."

There was a slight pause before Dr Seward spoke again. "Don't you think I want this, too? Don't you think I've been driven quite mad seeing the two of you together? But there's a right way and a wrong way to do it. We had a plan."

Her stepmother's voice held the patent whine that Ella had come to recognise when the woman was

8

trying to get her own way. "I know, Bertie," she said. "But I... I don't want to wait anymore. He had to go."

Ella clapped a hand over her mouth to stifle the gasp of horror and stumbled backwards. Heart pounding, she scurried along the hall into the library.

Her father was lying on the chaise longue, his dark grey hair slick with sweat. His waxy pallor and blue lips painted a grotesque image, but it was the ragged breaths that sawed in and out of his lungs that ripped the cry from her.

"Papa!" Ella snuffed out the candle and dropped to her knees next to his prone body. "Oh, Papa, what's wrong?"

His eyes rolled in his head, and he took a moment to focus on her. "There she is," he gasped, blue lips pulled back over his teeth in a distorted smile. "My girl." He lifted his hand as though to touch her, but he groaned in pain and clasped his middle again. "Oh, Ella, she's... done it... she said she would..."

Ella blinked back the tears, stroking his clammy head. "Hush, Father. Doctor Seward is here. I'll go and get him."

"No!" The hoarse cry froze her to the spot before she could rise. "No, my darling... he... it's too late..."

"Papa, please," she sobbed. "He'll help you. I'll fetch him now."

Henry's grip tightened around her hand. "No, Ella. Listen to me. You must run. She'll get you, too."

"You're not making sense, Papa."

"Uncle... James... go there. He'll help," Henry caught

his breath and released it with a belly-wrenching groan.

Why was he talking about his estranged brother? As far as Ella knew, they'd not spoken in years. "We'll talk about it later, Father."

"No, Ella, please, listen to me… you must…"

Speaking was painful for him, and she shook her head. "Papa, just let me get Doctor–"

"Ella?" Albert Seward loomed in the open doorway.

Ella spun around to face them. "Doctor Seward, my father! You must help him!"

Clara nudged the doctor out of the way. Ella saw the fury reflected in her eyes even as she advanced on her. "What are you doing awake, Ella? It's past your bedtime!"

"Past my…" She stared at her stepmother with incredulity. "What did you do to him, Clara?"

She saw the effect of her words when Clara stalled. Her hand fluttered to her throat. "I-I did nothing, Ella. How *dare* you speak to me like this!" Ella watched the anger ripple over her shock. "Mrs Green woke me. She was extinguishing the lights and found your father in here like this. I sent Willie to fetch Doctor Seward."

Ella's fists rolled into balls at her sides. Just a moment ago, she'd been calling him Bertie. "What's wrong with him?" She directed her question to the doctor who was hovering behind her. They didn't know she'd been in the doorway, and her mind raced ahead with trying to work out what all these adults were *not* saying.

Doctor Seward sighed and crossed to the mahogany desk that her father favoured so much. He reached into the bowl of water on it, wrung out a cloth and handed it to Clara. "Your father has been sick for a while, Ella. You know this. Clearly, his last work trip has taken its toll, even though I'd advised him against it."

Ella's eyes narrowed. It was true that her father had had a run of stomach problems, but he'd been fine at supper. He'd been his usual jovial self, even as they'd entertained their guests.

Clara dabbed at her husband's cheeks, crooning softly, "Oh, Henry, my love. Albert is here now. He says you're going to be fine."

Henry coughed. Clara reared back as she was sprayed with the blood-red foam. "Albert? What's happening?"

Doctor Seward pulled Clara out of the way. He was rolling back his sleeves, looking intently at her father. "You should wait in the hallway, Ella."

"I'm not going anywhere," Ella took a step forward, but Clara levelled a look at her.

"Get out!" She hissed. "You should be in bed, not traipsing about in the dark. I don't even know what you're doing out of bed."

"He's my father," Ella began.

"He's my *husband*," Clara snapped back. "For once in your wretched life, do as you are told."

"Come, child," Mrs Green, the housekeeper, stepped into the room. She placed her hands on Ella's shoulders and tried to guide her away from the grisly sight. "You don't need to see this. Come," she said again when Ella twisted out of her grip. "Let's wait in the kitchen, dear."

Ella hesitated. Her father's breathing was shallow and rapid, with foam collecting in the corners of his mouth. She gave in to the housekeeper's prompts. The last thing she saw as she looked back was the doctor and her stepmother looming over her father's prone form.

She allowed herself to be steered through the dimly lit house, down along the narrow passages, past the housekeeper's pantry and the still room until the warmth of the kitchen enveloped her.

The cooker filled the alcove in the wall to the right. Several bedsheets had been hung over thin rope along the roof to dry in the huge rectangle-shaped room. Copper pans hung on the walls, and rows of jars filled the shelves that ran along the back wall. An oak table dominated the centre of the space, its surface was almost white from years of being scrubbed by Mrs Green and her predecessors.

Milly looked up when they walked in and then finished pouring the hot water into a pot. Her expression softened when she met Ella's distraught expression, but she remained quiet.

Mrs Green pressed Ella down into one of the chairs next to it. "He'll be okay, Miss. You'll see. You know the travel makes your father sick. Mr Tomlinson is strong as an ox. Doctor Seward is the best there is," she said. "All this excitement will be over in the morning."

Ella sent Milly a watery thank you as a cup was

placed on the table. Strange how being in the kitchen with these ladies settled her nerves more than being seated in the grand dining room upstairs.

"I'm surprised to see you up at this hour." Mrs Green pulled a cup towards herself and let out a groan as she lowered her rump into another chair and absently rubbed at her knees. "Mrs Tomlinson said that she thought it best to wait until morning."

"I heard the commotion," Ella murmured without missing a beat or looking up. "I'm glad I did, else I would have slept on. Did my father eat anything unusual last night?"

Mrs Green looked affronted. "Cook prepared the meat in the same way that she always does. You ate the same food, too."

Ella rubbed a brow and sighed. "I didn't mean to imply anything untoward, Mrs Green. My father was holding his stomach and..." she rolled a hand in front of her face, "frothing at the mouth. Yet he was fine when we ate dinner."

The old housekeeper kept any further comments to herself though directed a look of annoyance at Milly as the maid clattered dishes into the sink. Before she could say another word, a chiming filled the kitchen. The three looked up at the call bell board. The bell marked 'study' moved.

Ella's heart dropped into her stomach, and she shot out of the door and up the narrow, steep stairs, ignoring the protests of the staff behind her. She slid to a halt when she saw Clara standing in front of the study door, fingers linked in front of her. Her expression was carefully schooled into contrition. Ella was vaguely aware of Mrs Green and Milly huffing up the staircase behind her.

"Father?"

Doctor Seward emerged from the study, wearing a similarly grim face. He shook his head. "I'm sorry, Ella. Your father has died."

CHAPTER 2

*B*eyond her bedroom window, Ella could see the grey rooftop tiles of the houses opposite that curved around the expanse of grass that separated the streets. The grey cobbled road was framed by a neat black iron fence. The honey-coloured limestone terraces appeared dour under the granite sky, the steady downpour suiting her mood as if the world outside her bedroom window cried, too.

The trees were still naked as winter fought to keep its icy grip on the lands, the distant rolling hills disappearing in the low-lying cloud.

She left her chair next to the window to add more coal to the fire. She waited for the flames to catch the fuel, standing in the centre of the room, and wondering what she was meant to do.

Carriages lined the street below, a steady stream of visitors lamenting the death of Henry Tomlinson. She'd been told to take solace in their shared grief, but she knew deep down that the death of her father meant that her life would never be the same again.

Her eyes lit upon the small rosewood and satin-wood cross-banded violin case; the lid ingrained with swirls of marquetry. Her fingers stretched out to gently stroke the smooth, polished surface as a gamut of memories slammed into her.

Her father had told the story about how her grandfather had been awarded the pretty case by a prestigious client after a successful legal battle. Ella didn't care how her grandfather came by it. It was her greatest possession. Holding her breath, she flipped back the brass hinges and opened the case. Within the crushed blue velvet bedding lay her father's violin.

She lifted out the violin, the scrolled wood tucking neatly between her shoulder and her chin as she lay the bow against the strings.

Her father had claimed that she'd derived from a long line of musicians, but the violin had always felt as if it was an extension of herself. As she drew the bow across the strings, her eyes drifted closed, and the soulful tune filled the bed chamber. A bittersweet smile touched her lips.

She had been taught to play an instrument from a young age. Her father had always insisted that it was the mark of a true lady, but she would have eagerly played regardless of its significance. Many evenings in the past had been spent in joyful harmony with her father, as they played the piano or violin together. Sometimes, she would simply sing along to the tunes he played. Now, standing in the middle of her bedroom, her hands moved instinctively as she lost herself in the music as if guided by an unseen force. The memory of her father's delighted face, as he watched her play, was as vivid as if he were still in the room with her. Without realising it, her face was wet with tears.

She was so entrenched that she wasn't aware that the door had opened, or that anybody was in the room until she heard Clara's voice screeching at her, "Where did you get that?"

Ella stumbled backwards, staring confusedly at her stepmother. Rage twisted the woman's face, and before Ella could say a word, Clara leapt upon her and snatched the violin out of her hands.

Even as Ella lunged for the instrument, Clara slapped at her, sending Ella sprawling across the room. Ella cried out in horror as Clara tossed the violin into the flames of the fire. She scrambled to her knees and cried out as she tried in vain to reach the hearth, but Clara was too strong for her.

"It isn't right that he let you play that wretched thing. I can't stand the sound that it makes. It's like listening to a cat calling in the gutter for its mate."

Hands outstretched, paralyzed by grief, Ella watched as the flames devoured her father's violin.

"Things are going to be a little different here now that I'm in charge," Clara said.

And with that, she stalked from the room and shut the door behind her.

"You should have woken me."

Thomas' words were muttered into his chest. Ella wondered if his red-rimmed eyes matched hers. With his head bowed, he looked much younger. His auburn hair fell across his forehead despite the oil that one of the maids must have applied. Although four years his senior, she often felt that the distance between them was made wider by Clara. Her brother was adored by his mother, something that he often used to torment Ella. His lighter colouring and brown eyes had always been a source of annoyance for him, but Clara had assured him he'd inherited his looks from his grandfather, a man who'd died long before Henry had ever met her.

The day had seemed interminable. The funeral invites had been delivered and Clara had insisted on making the list a long one. Ella had covered one of her good dresses in black crepe though it appeared her stepmother had purchased a new mourning dress.

The death of a prominent man like Henry Tomlinson meant that fellow barristers and advocates of the law, friends and extended family members had gathered at their home. Chairs had been arranged along the edges of the room, and Ella sat in one next to Thomas. The open casket had sat pride of place in the sitting room for those people to pay their respects, but Ella couldn't look upon her father without recalling his painful final moments. She wanted the coffin to be closed just so she didn't have to dwell on that grotesque memory.

Now, she looked at her brother, and her heart filled with sorrow for him. She knew what it was like to lose a parent already. Her mother had died when she was five. She reached out to clasp his hand. "Thomas, you must believe me when I tell you that seeing Papa that way isn't something that you'd want to have forever etched in your mind."

Thomas slowly pulled his hand back and Ella recoiled from the venom that fired his eyes. "You did it deliberately. Mother said she'd told you that you were to wake me, but you refused."

Ella shook her head, her mouth rounding in shock. "That simply isn't true, Thomas. I was woken by," she cut off the words before she could betray Milly and rolled her lips.

She sought out her stepmother across the room. Clara was with Doctor Seward and a man she didn't recognise. She looked every ounce of the widow as she dabbed the black-edged handkerchief to her eyes.

I decided to take things into my own hands.

Ella had heard the words that night. She played them over and over in her mind, trying to work out their meaning. She knew that her father and Clara could have terrific arguments. More than once, she'd heard porcelain smashing as Clara had lost her temper. It made Ella nervous, knowing that she could lose control like that yet be so utterly serene in the next breath.

She'd hoped that her stepmother might end the competition that she seemed to incite in her son now that Henry was gone, but hearing what she'd said to Thomas quashed that dream. Ella loved her brother and longed for a harmonious relationship with him. Henry had told her that it would happen once Thomas was older and could make his own choices, but Ella wasn't so sure. Henry hadn't been home all that much. He didn't know the depths his young wife could stoop to when the mood took her.

Would Clara have done something to her husband? She was looking at the woman through a different lens now, even as she tried to reason away what she'd heard that night. Albert Seward had been her companion ever since Henry's death and Ella watched them together.

Don't you think I want this, too?

She couldn't remember a time when Doctor Seward hadn't been her father's friend. She'd assumed they'd met when her mother had been so sick because Dr Seward treated patients with cancer. He'd even been at their house the night Thomas had been born, helping bring her brother into the world.

"You were woken by?" Thomas' hissed question interrupted her thoughts.

She looked back at him and reminded herself that he was as grief-stricken as she was, and still a child. "I had no idea Papa was so sick else of course I would have woken you."

Thomas tilted his head, eyes narrowed in a manner

that had Clara reflected in them. "You've always been jealous of me. That I stand to inherit everything, and you are just a woman."

The spiteful tone hurt. "Thomas, you are my brother," she whispered tearfully. "One day, it will just be the two of us. Please, your mother must be mistaken about what happened. She didn't tell me to wake you."

The movement of the pallbearers drowned out her words. Ella watched as the coffin was finally closed and she felt the finality of his loss as keenly as a knife to the skin. Her father had been the mediator between Thomas, Clara, and Ella. No matter how hard Ella had tried, she always knew that she was the cuckoo in the nest.

She rose silently, uncaring that her grief was visible to the mourners. The casket was draped with a velvet blanket and carried from the room and out to the waiting hearse. Clara had spared no expense. The black carriage burgeoned with flowers and ostrich feathers, and the six black horses pulling it were as elaborately dressed in matching feathers. A variety of foot attendants lined the street, and the procession formed a sea of black as it rolled resolutely towards the cemetery.

Ella followed Clara, Thomas, and Doctor Seward, the three of them leading the group. The rain fell softly, clouds of mist muffling the slow marching steps. Her brother's sobs echoed her own quiet sniffles, and she felt a twist of envy when she saw the Doctor put his arm around Thomas in comfort.

Her father had always been the one to offer her

comfort. She'd tried her best to make Clara happy over the years, but she'd never quite matched the expectations. Now, Ella had lost the one person she'd relied on for guidance and support. He'd always been a willing ear when he was home, which had been less and less of late.

Clara had already begun to create a bigger fissure in the relationship that Ella had with her brother. After all, Thomas was the only link that she had left to her father. Henry Tomlinson had been proud of his children, and he made no bones about the fact that Thomas was to follow in his footsteps into law one day. She wanted to tell her father about the lie that Clara had told Thomas, to have him speak to Thomas over the bitterness she'd seen in his eyes. She'd remembered the utter happiness of having a little brother; her father had announced that a sibling was a blessing and that he'd enjoyed many a happy memory with his brother. What would she do if she lost Thomas, too?

Ella saw the hole yawning in the ground as she passed through the wide stone gates to the cemetery. This pitiful ending didn't feel right for a man as vibrant and dynamic as her father had been. She wasn't supposed to watch the interment. It was only meant for the men to attend but she refused to be pulled away from his coffin when she still had so much that she wanted to say to him, to learn from him.

She tried to resist the cajoling from the mourners, but it was Clara's vice-like grip on her upper arm that cut through her fog of hurt. She wasn't given any choice but to wait with the other women. Up ahead, she could see Thomas at the graveside, with Dr Seward next to him. It didn't seem fair that the men could say a final goodbye, but she couldn't.

"Don't you show me up now," Clara hissed at her. "You'll wait here, as is the right way."

Ella flinched from the words and kept her eyes down. "I'm sorry."

"You're always sorry."

Ella looked at the exquisite profile of her stepmother.

He had to go.

The whispered conversation she'd overheard drifted through her mind. The doctor would know what to give a man to make him sick, but Henry had had stomach problems for months leading up to that night. Confusion twisted her thoughts. Still, there was one thing that she wanted to know from her stepmother.

"Why isn't Uncle James here?"

CHAPTER 3

*E*lla saw surprise slide over Clara's carefully rouged face. "Why would that ruffian be here?"

"Papa would have wanted him here. They're brothers."

Clara snorted derisively. "Your father hadn't spoken to James in years, Ella. I wouldn't even know where he lived now to be able to tell him."

"But he's family."

Clara cocked her head, eyes hardening as she peered down her narrow nose. "No, he isn't. He was a drunken lout who brought shame onto the Tomlinson name. Your father wanted nothing to do with him."

In his final moments, James had been the one on Henry's mind. She knew that her father would have wanted him here. "You're wrong."

Clara huffed out a mirthless laugh. "Are you trying to tell me that I don't know my own husband? I told

24

you that there will be some changes around here now, Ella."

Impotent rage twined with her grief. She'd burned her most prized possession for no reason. The loss of her violin had felt as if she'd lost the one tangible connection she'd had to her father. She blinked and her tears spilt down her cheeks.

"The staff and I are heading back to the house, Mrs Tomlinson," Mrs Green interrupted Clara's inevitable tirade. "We'll get the food laid out ready."

"Of course," Clara replied stiffly. "I shall wait in the carriage for Thomas and Doctor Seward. Ella, you can walk back with Mrs Green."

Ella's eyes widened but any argument she voiced was dismissed with a black-gloved hand. Clara picked her way across the loose stones to the waiting hansom.

"Miss?" Milly called Ella. The servants were huddled under umbrellas, dressed in black. Willie, the hall boy, wore a coat that was too long in the sleeves. Milly beckoned to her and waited for her as Ella cast one final look back at the cemetery.

Mrs Green and the cook made their way along the pavements, back the way they'd come. Ella slowly filed behind them.

"Mrs Tomlinson has a lot on her plate right now," Milly said quietly. "Once everything has settled, things will go back to normal."

"They won't, Milly. I fear that my stepmother has an agenda that only she knows about."

Ella didn't say anything more. No one else had been

privy to the conversation that had taken place in the library. Sleep had eluded her most nights as she'd pondered the meaning. But she had an idea that her father warning her to leave held more sway than she'd given it credit. Clara was already setting the wheels in motion for where her place would be in this new life. She looked ahead to the housekeeper and was struck by an idea.

She waited until the staff had all been given their tasks to stoke the fires and set out the grand buffet in the parlour, leaving her alone in the servant's hall with the housekeeper.

"Mrs Green, may I ask you something?"

The housekeeper peered at her. "Make it quick, child. Mrs Tomlinson and the party will be back soon."

"How long have you worked for my father?"

"For more years than I can count on my fingers and toes." The answer made her smile. "My father knew him, my Ma, too. He was a good employer; no fairer man ever walked the earth. I hope to be able to hold onto the position."

Ella blinked. "Why on earth would you think you wouldn't be kept on?"

The query flustered her. Her cheeks puffed out with agitation. She was hooking the ring with all the keys to the townhouse to her belt, resuming her duties. "I-I don't mean anything by it, Miss. It's just... Mrs Tomlinson is a young woman still. Your father will no doubt have left her a wealthy woman, but she is the head of this house now." Her kind eyes settled on Ella's face. "She will warm to you once her heart has healed from her grief."

Ella digested the information that had sent the older woman flapping. Ella shook her head, returning to her earlier point before Mrs Green had reached the door.

"Do you remember my father's brother?"

She could tell that the question was an unexpected one. Mrs Green halted in the doorway. "Y-yes, I do," she stammered.

"Did my father quarrel with him?"

Mrs Green's eyes slid towards the ceiling as if checking they weren't being overheard.

"It's not my place to speak about such matters, Miss Ella."

"I'm sorry if this puts you in an awkward position, Mrs Green. My father mentioned him that night… before he…"

"I'm led to believe that they rowed, yes, miss. I don't know the cause, nor should I," the housekeeper added sternly.

"Do you know where my Uncle James is?"

Mrs Green sighed deeply. "No, Ella. Mrs Tomlinson only invited the people whom your father loved and who respected him. You saw how many people there were. Take comfort in that, if you can."

The doorbell rang and the housekeeper hurried away to tend to the visitors. Ella trudged up the stairs behind her, determined to hold her head up high and pay her respects to her father one last time. She saw Doctor Seward handing his coat and hat to Milly. He smiled when he saw her emerging from the rear staircase.

"Ella, you walked home?"

"Yes, doctor," she dropped her gaze to hide her perplexity. She saw his shoes appear in her line of sight as he came closer.

"I know things seem difficult for you now, but you shouldn't worry." His tone seemed genuine though she couldn't bring herself to meet his eyes.

"I shan't, doctor."

"Good. You'll see, things will get better soon enough. I made your father a promise that I would take care of you and Thomas."

Her eyes lifted at that. What had happened in those moments when Clara had banished her from the room as her father had writhed in agony? What had been his last words? Thomas was undoubtedly hurt by being denied the chance to say goodbye to his father, but Ella, too, had been excluded from those final few words from Henry Tomlinson.

She'd trusted Doctor Seward to save her father and he hadn't. But would he have, even if he could? She searched his face for falsehoods, but his expression remained unreadable. "What were you treating my father for?"

"I beg your pardon?"

Ella took advantage of his discomfiture from her direct question. "You told me yourself the night he died that you'd been treating him for months. I asked Papa and he said that you'd been running tests. What was it that was making him poorly?"

His eyes darted around the hallway before they settled in one spot. Ella didn't have to look to know that he was seeking out Clara. "Ella, you shouldn't be speaking about this. Not today, of all days."

"When then?" Ella pressed, hearing the clip of Ella's boots on the polished parquet flooring.

"Doctor Seward, may I speak with you privately?" Clara spoke, laying a hand along his forearm.

"I want to know what was wrong with my father," Ella tried again but baulked when Clara leaned in.

"Ella, you're upset. And you're making our guests uncomfortable. I think it's best if you go to your room." Clara's tone was affectionate but that belied the malice shining in her eyes. "Thomas is already upstairs. The interment took its toll on him. Perhaps you could look in on him for me."

"He won't speak to me," Ella whispered, her voice thick with emotion. Wherever she turned, she was met with resistance.

"Please,' Clara tacked on servilely.

Ella divided a look between the pair and then turned for the stairs. She left the chattering behind, the dull ache in her chest increasing when Thomas refused to open his bedroom door. She climbed to the upper floor. Her room had chilled; the fire having been neglected by the maids as they tended to the more important task of keeping up appearances. She set about reviving it and washed the coal dust off in the bowl of water in the corner whilst far below, people celebrated the life of her father.

CHAPTER 4

*E*lla heard the footsteps approaching her room long before the brass doorknob to her bedroom rattled. The one benefit to having a floor to herself meant that she was usually forewarned when Clara or Thomas was approaching, though it was Milly's face that appeared in the gap as soon as the door opened.

Ella marked her page with a ribbon and closed the book. "Good morning, Milly."

Milly slipped through the door and pressed it closed by leaning against it. "Pardon my interrupting, miss," she said. "But I wonder if I may have a word."

"Of course," Ella replied, as a lick of trepidation kicked at her heartbeat. "Why do you look so worried?"

Milly's hands knotted together in front of her as the maid's eyes danced around the room.

Ella's brows crunched together. "Milly?"

"Mrs Green would have my guts for garters if she

knew I was in here," Milly said quickly. She took a small step further into the room. "Cook has herself in a right tizzy. She's gone to pay the coal man for the delivery this morning, but the housekeeper's tin was as empty as Cook's tin is.

Mrs Green's already put a request in to draw some money out but didn't want to bother Mrs Tomlinson about it on account of what's been happening with Mr Tomlinson an' all. Cook says it don't look right, a big house like this running up debts and how she never did it when Mr Tomlinson was here. First of the month," her head bobbed with certainty. "Mr Tomlinson would check with the staff that they had what they needed. If he was on his travels, it would be taken care of and now…"

Ella rose and placed reassuring hands on Milly's narrow shoulder as she tried to pick out the hurried words. "Okay," she said soothingly. "It may be that Clara has just overlooked the problem. I'll speak to her."

Milly almost sagged with relief. "Thank you, miss, I knew that you would understand. I best get back downstairs before they know I am missing."

Ella smiled and waited for the young maid to hurry from the room before she readied herself to face her stepmother. Ella didn't know anything about the finances of the house. It wasn't a woman's place to know such things. But maybe, she mused as she left her bedroom, that rule was made up by somebody who hadn't considered people being widowed.

She found Clara in the parlour, with an array of papers spread out on the dining table in front of her. Her carefully formulated questions died on her lips when Clara looked up with her at her with abject misery.

For a moment, Clara stared at her stepdaughter. Ella hesitated at the threshold of the door and sent the other woman an attentive smile.

"Good morning."

"Is it?" Clara demanded.

Ella momentarily put aside her concerns about her father's accounts. "Is there something I can help you with?" she asked hesitantly.

Clara released a heavy sigh. "We're broke," she announced with a flourish of her hands, indicating the spread of papers before her.

Ella stared, momentarily stunned. Her father had been a highly successful businessman. They lived in a grand house on the edge of town, she wore beautiful clothes, and they had a staff of servants. "I don't know what you mean."

"What I mean is, your father had everyone fooled. For years, he had me believe that he was rich when he wasn't! He convinced me that he was prosperous when he was an imbecile. I've had those idiots from below demanding money from me to pay the coalmen this morning, and the truth of it is there's no money left in the account. Your father has left us penniless!"

Ella crossed the floor, tilting her head to get a better look at the papers. Clara pushed them toward her roughly so that they fluttered to the floor around her feet.

"Take a look for yourself if you don't believe me," she snapped.

Ella bent and attempted to collect the papers, but the facts and figures they contained made no sense to her inexperienced eyes. "There must be some kind of mistake," she said.

"There isn't!" Clara screamed at her as she stood and leaned across the polished table. "He made a foolhardy investment that I knew nothing about until the day of his funeral when one of his business connections mentioned it. I thought the man had lost his mind when he was rambling on about how investing in a mine somewhere that no one's ever heard of was the worst idea your father had ever had.

It turns out your father was reckless! A reckless idiot with no thought of the future. What are we to do? What am I to do?" Clara sank back into her seat and covered her face as she sobbed.

Ella placed the papers on the table, torn between wanting to defend her father and the desperation evident in Clara's voice. "I can't believe that Father would have done something like this. He said he was always so careful."

"Your father was a lot of things that you never knew about," Clara spat, lowering her hands to glare balefully at her.

"It's not all lost. We can sell this house," Ella began,

but Clara stared at her as if she had suddenly grown a second head.

"Have you taken leave of all of what little sense you had? My son cannot be displaced from what is rightfully *his* home. What a ridiculous notion!"

Ella clamped her mouth shut as Clara's angry words struck her like blows. She seemed only concerned about the effects on Clara and Thomas and hadn't once mentioned what Ella was going to do. "Try not to worry," Ella said. "I'm sure if you spoke to one of Father's business partners, they would be able to look through these papers and have a better understanding."

"Do you think I'm some kind of simpleton?" Clara demanded. "I can read, Ella. I can do simple math. There is no money. We are broke!"

With that, Clara stormed from the room, slamming the door behind her for good measure. The gust of air sent the papers fluttering again onto the floor. Ella bent down to pick up the papers and took a seat. She couldn't believe that her father would risk everything and leave his family, or himself, broke. He wouldn't have expected to die.

She read through the papers one by one – account ledgers, bank certificates, and letters that had arrived from overseas informing her father of the losses of his investments. Letters from the bank explained that the property had to be mortgaged to cover the loss of his investment.

The letters and the figures scrawled on the paper in front of her blurred as tears filled her eyes. It seemed that even as the daughter of a successful barrister who had a long history of business acumen behind him, her father had made a poor investment. Ella wondered if financial worries had been the cause of the many arguments between Clara and her father. It all seemed very complicated, and she wanted to get someone else's opinion, someone who had more understanding of what she was looking at.

She bundled the papers up intending to check her father's office when the doorbell rang. A quick look through the window showed that Dr Seward's carriage was outside, and he was standing at the front door waiting to be let in. Ella crept across to the door, lightly cracking it open so she could hear.

"Oh, Bertie!" Clara howled.

Ella's frown deepened as she was reminded of the conversation that she'd overheard the night her father had died.

"I got your note from the hall boy. Whatever is the matter, Clara?" Dr Seward's voice was laced with concern, and Ella pictured the two of them embracing. She parted the door slightly to peek, but they weren't touching.

"Oh, it's hopeless!" Clara dissolved into tears, and Ella watched as the doctor indeed wrapped an arm around her stepmother's shoulders. He then clicked his fingers at Milly and instructed the young maid to bring some tea into the drawing room. The door shut firmly, cutting off any further opportunity to eavesdrop.

Paperwork forgotten, Ella hurried up the stairs.

There had to be a mistake. Henry Tomlinson wasn't a man who made risky decisions. She decided that she would write to the two men that her father worked with. She explained what she had seen as best as she could and asked them to advise her on what steps to take next.

She took the letters and went down the stairs to ask Milly to post them when she was next out until she remembered that there was no money in the house-keeper's office to pay the coalman, let alone to buy any penny stamps.

Instead, she turned to her father's study. Her hand touched the door handle and had to catch her breath against the sudden onslaught of memories that washed over her. Her father had been in the ground less than a month and yet they were so fresh, leaving her feeling raw and upset.

As a tree fall, so shall it lie.

She squeezed her eyes shut tight when she heard the echo of her father's voice in the recesses of her mind. The words were murmured to her when she'd cried in his arms, asking God for her mother.

Life goes on, my sweet girl, Henry had murmured to her, stroking her hair as he'd held her to him. *Your mother would want you to make her proud by being good and kind, which you are every day.*

She set her shoulders back and opened the door, studiously ignoring the sofa on which her father had lain. She crossed to his walnut writing table, searching the contents of the drawers as hastily as she could.

Pens, ink, envelopes… she wished now that she'd paid more attention to where her father may keep his money.

No stamps, no money.

Thinking that she could simply ask the postmaster to pay for the stamps at the end of the month like the housekeeper did with most things, she shut the bottom drawer, but it caught on something. A couple more tries to close it were unsuccessful. With an exasperated sigh, she dropped to her knees and twisted her hand to reach towards the back of the drawer to free whatever was blocking it.

Her fingers brushed what had caught and she tugged it forward. A bundle of letters tied together with twine. She settled the packet back in place so that she was able to fully close the drawer and pressed it down when she saw the name in the corner of the top letter.

Her heart slowly tripped over itself, and she snatched up the packet, her mouth parting with a gasp.

James.

CHAPTER 5

"***W***hat were you doing in there?"

Ella whirled and swallowed her yelp. Her brother was in the hallway. He folded his arms and lifted a brow in question. She surreptitiously wiped her damp palms on her skirts, the letters that she'd discovered having been hidden in the folds.

"It soothes me, Thomas." She cast her eyes down even as her pulse hammered in her veins. Would he even care that their uncle might want to know about the death of his brother? Surely, there was significance in her father hiding letters so well. She needed to go to her room and read them.

"You shouldn't be in there. It was Papa's domain. Mother wouldn't like it."

Ella raised her eyes and offered him a soft smile. She prayed that her brother wouldn't notice her eagerness to go upstairs. "I know. I hope that you won't mention this. Your mother has enough on her mind right now. I wouldn't want to burden her more."

Thomas's shoulders lifted indifferently. "Soon enough, you can sneak about to your heart's content. I have my own adventures to plan."

Ella caught the excitement shimmering in his eyes. "What do you mean?"

"Mother has heard from the school," he clapped in glee. "I am to start there next month."

Her father has always hoped that his only boy would follow in his footsteps into law. It had been a great source of pride for him. Ella's smile was spontaneous and warm.

"Thomas, that's wonderful. You shall make a fine barrister, I'm certain."

Her brother recoiled, eyes wide and he shook his head, his smile smug. "I'm not going to Rugby, Ella. Mother has told me that I am enrolled at Eton."

Ella sighed, unwilling to be the bearer of bad news. Her brother had his dreams, too. Dreams that would no doubt be affected now that the coffers were empty. Opportunities that would be hindered by having no money to pay for an education in an establishment such as Eton.

"Thomas, I'm not sure that going to such a fine school will be possible for you anymore. You're a bright lad; you'll flourish in any school you attend, and Eton's fees would normally be a stretch at the best of times. Moreso now.

You've had the best start and I'm certain that Papa's

associates will see to it that you find gainful employment at a fine law firm when the time comes."

"I'm not studying law," he scoffed.

"I thought that that's what you wanted to do?"

He gave her a pitying head shake, so reticent of his mother that it sent shivers along Ella's spine. "No, Ella. I'm going to be a doctor. After Eton, I will go to Edinburgh."

"A doctor? But… what about the agreement you made with Papa?"

"Those were his dreams, never mine. Doctor Seward says that he will give me a letter of recommendation. Having such a glowing reference will serve me well in the medical field."

Ella's heart hurt a little bit more. Her father had been so proud of his son and now, it seemed almost as soon as her father's back was turned, Thomas was reneging on his word. She was sure that her father would be heartbroken.

Thomas' laugh was scathing when she voiced her fears. "Doctor Seward is a respected doctor, Ella. Mother says I'd be a fool to turn down such an opportunity."

"Thomas," Ella hedged, gnawing at her lower lip until she realised that there was no kind way to say what needed to be said. "We simply don't have the money to send you to school."

There was that laugh again. Ella had to grit her teeth to clamp off the angry words.

"Doctor Seward says that we do not need to worry about the money."

Ella's eyes drifted past Thomas to the closed drawing-room door. Clara hadn't been in any fit state to break the news to her son that his dreams must change. Ella knew first-hand just how unpredictable Clara could be and she had no desire to expose Thomas to Clara's fits of rage.

"Thomas. Sometimes in life, things don't always go to plan. The truth is that Papa... well, we have a bigger change in circumstances than we first thought. We might have to move–"

Thomas' face turned red as his fists balled at his sides. "I am going to school!" He shouted at her. "Doctor Seward and Mother told me this just now!"

The door behind her brother opened and Clara's frowning face filled the gap it made. "What on earth are you two arguing about – in the hallway, no less? We have staff!" she hissed at them, the focus of her anger on Ella standing next to Thomas.

Ella's fingers knotted together. "I was trying to explain to Thomas what you were telling me earlier. About how he must change his plans now that we have no money."

Clara's thin lips disappeared as her mouth flattened. "You will stop this instant with such lies, Ella! Thomas' education is of paramount importance to your father, and therefore to me."

"I know this, but you told me that we had–"

"I don't know what game you're playing, Ella, but it stops this instant."

Ella's argument died on her lips, confusion filling her. Perhaps she was denying the truth to save face in front of her son, or Doctor Seward who emerged through the door.

"Perhaps now is the time to tell her," The doctor suggested quietly.

Clara looked back at him for a moment before she smiled. It was the most beatific smile and Ella could now see why Henry indulged the other woman so much. "I wanted to do this more officially, Ella," she began, barely able to conceal the happiness that radiated from her. "But your wretched insolence means that I have to alter my plans once again."

"I don't follow."

"Well, of course, you don't," Clara said in a haughty tone. "You rarely follow anything. Doctor Seward has secured a place for Thomas at a very elite school. He will cover the monies required for your brother to attend there."

Ella caught the victorious look Thomas was giving her. Envy, fierce and bright, curled sinuously through her insides. It was an ugly emotion but one that she couldn't help. Thomas was given so many more opportunities than she could ever hope for simply because he was male. Her education had been given by a Governess who smelled of eggs and had fast hands if she made a mistake with any of her three R's. He could now escape this home and experience so many more things thanks to his generous benefactor, whereas her future was even more uncertain.

"That's incredibly considerate, Doctor Seward. I know my father would appreciate your altruistic kindness towards my brother."

The doctor cleared his throat and stepped further into the hall. He looked at Clara and held her warm gaze. "He's a very bright young man, full of promise."

"Thank you, Doctor Seward," Thomas replied, blossoming under the high praise.

Doctor Seward aligned himself between Clara and Thomas. Her brother was almost as tall as the doctor stood; his rangy body was vastly different from the portly stature of Henry Tomlinson. Ella's brows knitted as her eyes moved along the three of them, an immutable wall of solidarity.

Thomas' brown eyes were lit with triumph, and they were so similar to the man's standing right next to him. Her frown deepened as uneasiness boiled in her gut. Echoes of whispered words drifted through her mind, and she looked upon the three of them with eyes anew.

Don't you think I've been driven quite mad seeing the two of you together?

"Say something, Ella, don't just stare at us all as if you're at the circus."

Ella's mouth flapped as the unthinkable bloomed in her mind. She felt as though the mists had cleared and suddenly the susurrations that she'd heard that night were now abundantly clear. Thomas was like the doctor in so many ways – why had she never seen it before? Even as her eyes made the comparisons, her stuttering mind refused to believe such a discovery. Thomas was her brother... wasn't he?

"Should I tell her the rest?" Clara sought permission from Albert. The doctor inclined his head after a moment's hesitation.

Caught up in the horror of what her eyes were finally seeing, Ella swung her gaze to Clara. "Tell me what?"

Clara's beaming smile was illuminated once more when the Doctor caught Clara by the hands. His attention was focused entirely on her when he spoke, "Clara has agreed to become my wife."

CHAPTER 6

eth

"Thank you, John," Seth Milford hopped down from the carriage, the gravel crunching under his boots.

The driver tipped his hat and shut the carriage door behind him. Seth tugged at the fingertips of his gloves, his long strides carrying him up across the sandy driveway of Linton Manor and up the crescent-shaped stone steps.

The grey stone Georgian house was built in Palladium style, the golden Corinthian pillars of the entrance porch forming the centre of the symmetrical design. The white shutters were thrown open to the warm spring sunshine so that the Milford family and guests could admire the neatly manicured lawns and foliage that was the work of John and his team of gardeners. Beyond the black iron fencing were the rolling hills of the countryside.

"Good afternoon, Master Seth," Mr Dwyer, the stout butler held the door open. The man was formal and proper, clearly proud of his station in such a fine English home.

"Hello, Dwyer," Seth handed his gloves off to Andrew, the young footman, with a murmured thanks. Another young boy set the cases at Seth's feet and was summarily dismissed by the butler.

As much as he hadn't wanted to return for this party, he had to admit that it was nice to be home. The interior of the elegant house showed off the wealth of the Milfords. The grand hall that they stood in was dominated by a sweeping staircase that curved up to a mezzanine floor, its polished oak bannisters and hand-carved spindles gleaming in the light that shone through the wide windows. The walls were soft muted shades of blue and green, offset by white mouldings and ceiling roses, with a huge chandelier that had once belonged to a Duke. The floors were covered in plush carpets, the intricate patterns in contrast to the graceful lines of the mahogany furniture that filled the space.

He'd made a comfortable life for himself at the family townhouse in Regent's Park. It was convenient for travelling to his office in the Albert Dock, which allowed him to enjoy a healthy social life. The townhouse was moderately furnished which suited Seth better.

For the most part, he had the townhouse to himself as his father, Philip Milford, preferred to return to the comfort of his grand manor house.

"Where is everyone?" Seth asked as he added his coat to the pile of clothing the footman held.

Dwyer closed the door, and stood ramrod straight, answering Seth although his eyes were on a spot somewhere behind Seth. "Your father is in the library. Your mother was resting upstairs. Master Giles is yet to arrive, and your sister is with Mr Donovan in the parlour."

Seth paused. "My sister is here?"

Dwyer inclined his head slowly. "Yes, sir."

"Golly, the stops truly have all been pulled out for this dinner party. I suppose I shall have to show willingness for this wretched inconvenience then," he groused.

"Andrew will valet for you, sir."

Seth sighed. "Really, Dwyer, that isn't necessary. I manage perfectly well at the townhouse with just Mrs Stewart and a housemaid. I can dress myself."

The butler's nostrils flared even wider, the only outward sign of his irritation at Seth's ongoing refusal to conform to societal rules. "At Linton Manor, your father thankfully insists on the proper way of doing things."

"And we wouldn't want to start the evening off with a quarrel just yet, would we?" Seth muttered. "Very well. I shall freshen up and then join my father before dinner."

Seth took the stairs two at a time. His bedroom was a haven of comfort and refinement, with richly patterned wallpaper and heavy-velvet curtains. His clothing for the evening's event had been set out on his bed ready, and Seth had to tamp down on the lick of irritation. He knew that he had to join in these point-less events; that cultivating business relationships and socialising were as much a part of what they did for a living as the global shipping of the cargo was. But it had always been his father's forte. For years, Seth was sick of being foisted into the limelight as the firstborn son and heir to the Milford fortune.

He was fed up with having simpering women trotted through the manor house in a matchmaking attempt by his parents. He knew that his refusal to find a wife and settle down was as baffling as it was irri-tating to them.

The bedroom was dominated by the four-poster bed, its dark wood frame intricately carved with swirling vines and leaves and draped in sumptuous silks. The bed linen was crisp and white, with a coverlet at the foot of the bed. A huge wall of pillows filled the top part. Seth thought the bed was ridicu-lously flamboyant, and much preferred his simpler bed at home.

As he stripped down, he wondered when he'd started to think of Regent's Park as being home. Sarah, Seth's mother, had been furious when he started spending more time in the city. For a while, his father Philip had supported the decision, as it brought Seth closer to his work. Philip was also aware that Seth had a keen interest in women who didn't necessarily belong to the same social circles or share the same wealthy status as the Milford family. However, when Philip tried to get Seth to settle down, his son outright refused.

Seth's social life had caused a great many arguments between him and his parents. Philip and Sarah Milford adhered to a strict moral code in their daily lives. Sarah believed that a woman's role was to manage the household, maintain her immaculate appearance, and raise the children appropriately. She enjoyed wearing the latest fashions and hosting international guests connected to her husband's shipping company.

While Sarah took care of the house and their daughter's upbringing, the boys had been sent away to school. Philip's responsibility was to earn money and make business deals.

Seth looked up when Andrew knocked at the door and walked in. He didn't even apologise for making a start on dressing himself. Seth knew that the servants in the manor house took great pride in their work, but he also realised that they would likely complain to the butler about his independent actions. While Seth didn't look down on anyone making an honest living, he would have preferred a lifestyle where servants weren't paraded around like status symbols for his father's guests.

He made small talk with the young man, asking after the servants and their families. It took a team of more than twenty servants to keep the manor house ticking over, plus more businesses in the nearby village that relied on the manor house for regular income.

The dinner gong had sounded by the time Andrew was fixing cufflinks to Seth's shirt. His suit was black and formal, as was expected of the people who attended these grand events at the manor house. The cook would have spent the best part of a fortnight planning, preparing, and cooking for the evening's fare. He checked his appearance in the full-length mirror in the wardrobe door.

"I look like a peacock," he sighed.

Andrew's lips twitched. "I think the term they use these days is handsome, sir."

His dark hair was suitably styled off his face, the high collar stiff against his neck. "Let's get this over with. The sooner it's done, the sooner I can get back to normal."

The footman disappeared back along the hallway. Even from the mezzanine level, Seth could already hear the hum of voices emanating from the drawing room. He made his way down the stairs, his irritation spiking as he pressed open the door.

The drawing room was the nucleus of functions at the manor house. The smooth white marble mantle-piece took pride of place, its neo-classical style matching the overstuffed sofas and fine armchairs upholstered in luxurious fabrics. The mahogany and cherrywood sideboards were crowded with gilded candlesticks and porcelain figures. A John Constable landscape hung over the hearth, depicting the rolling Suffolk countryside in which the manor house stood. Persian carpets were scattered across the floors, adding a pop of colour to the gleaming wooden surfaces.

His mother's invitation demanded his attendance tonight, stating that they had important guests staying for the weekend. Seth had assumed, wrongly it now appeared, that his new American brother-in-law, William Donovan, had finally come through on bringing some business into the company.

It seemed that his presence was expected here – but not to smooth the way into negotiating a shipping contract with an American trade firm. Instead, now that his sister Prudence was settled with her new beau, it appeared Sarah had once again turned her match-making attention back onto Seth.

He met and held his mother's gaze, catching the warning look that spoke volumes as she approached him.

"Hello, Mother," Seth murmured. He bussed his cheek to hers and was enveloped in her favourite rose perfume. Sarah Milford was an attractive woman, with intelligent brown eyes that she'd passed on to each of her children.

"Seth," she murmured. "I'm glad you made it."

He accepted the glass of wine that was handed to him. "I was left with very little choice and now, looking around the room, I can see that I've been outfoxed and manipulated." He kept his voice low so as not to carry but made sure that his tone let his mother know that he'd not changed his mind over her meddling in his affairs.

"It was your father's idea."

"Sarah, stop monopolising your son! Seth, come over here. I want to introduce you to someone." Philip Milford was the epitome of a successful entrepreneur. His sharp mind and keen nose had steered Milford Shipping to the powerhouse it was today. What had started as a small tugboat by Seth's grandfather in Portsmouth was now a fleet of steamships that connected the globe. But his father hadn't gotten to his position by accident. Philip Milford knew what he wanted for his family, and nothing would deviate from that plan.

"Seth," Philip extended a hand and Seth noted the way that the dark-haired man by his father's side was looking at him.

But it was the petite blonde woman at the stranger's arm that made the hairs on the back of Seth's neck rise. She was watching him with unbridled curiosity. Her dress was immaculate, as were the glossy curls that were piled upon her head. Seth placed her around her early twenties. Her style spoke of the highest fashion, from the exquisite silk that hugged her slender frame to the matching sapphires that flashed at her throat and ears.

"Denis, this is my son, Seth Milford." Seth caught the hand and gave it a firm shake, keeping his expression neutral. "Seth, this is Denis Harrison."

The keen young woman was staring at him long

after Seth had broken the look. "Good evening, sir. It's nice to meet you."

"Your father has just been telling me about the acquisition you've secured with a company in the Indies."

"That's right." Seth allowed his puzzlement to show through. "Though that deal was a cautious one until a few days ago."

"Denis here owns warehouses in Maine and New York."

"New Brunswick, too," Denis added proudly.

Seth already knew where this was going. They were always looking for storage on the other side of the Atlantic. All too often, the cargo would disappear off the quayside. Whether it was a careless captain or a cunning sailor looking to make a few extra pounds, their biggest money worry, after a ship sinking, was a loss of cargo once it reached land.

"Then we should talk," Seth said, happy that his father seemed to want to keep the talk to business this evening.

"But Papa," the blonde woman pouted. "You promised that there would not be any silly boat talk tonight."

Seth watched as Denis wilted under his daughter's question. "Of course not, my dear. Sorry, Seth, this is my daughter, Ophelia Harrison."

"Ophelia has come up, especially for the weekend," Sarah materialised by Seth's arm.

"I was in Bath for a few days, taking in the water

cure," Ophelia breathed. "It was sublime. Have you ever tried it, Mr Milford?"

Seth shook his head, feeling the pressure of all three parents watching him carefully, though it was the possessive look from Ophelia that made his collar feel tighter. "Can't say as I have."

"You have no idea what you're missing out on."

Sarah leaned in and gave him one of her pointed glares before she hooked her husband by the elbow and manoeuvred him and Denis away from the hearth, leaving Seth alone and defenceless with the young girl.

Ophelia's gleaming eyes turned predatory as she slipped a gloved hand over his forearm. "Now that they're out the way," she breathed. "We can speak freely."

Seth's eyes sought out his parents, furious that he'd been manipulated to babysit. Even Prudence was gloating at him from where she was perched on the corner of a tightly stuffed sofa. "What would you care to speak about?"

She giggled, covering her pointy little teeth as she laughed. "About our wedding, of course."

CHAPTER 7

lla

ELLA LEANED back against her bedroom door until the lock clicked back into place. A shuddering breath left her body as the ramifications of this discovery washed over her.

Although her mind struggled to grasp what her eyes had seen, she still couldn't quite believe that Clara would be so entirely devious. And now, they were to be *married*? Her father had barely been in the ground for a month. She knew that Clara wasn't much for tradition but even for her, this was outlandish.

Had her father known that Thomas wasn't his child? Anguish ripped through her, and she realised that it must've been tenfold for her poor father if he'd made the discovery. He'd never treated Thomas any differently to her, yet she couldn't help but wonder if he'd taken that secret to his grave.

She pressed her shaking fingers to her bloodless lips to try and contain her sobs. They were expecting her down for dinner, but how could she sit across from the table from these people and celebrate the good news after what she had learned? She quickly turned the key in her bedroom door and decided that she would forgo this evening's meal. She would be no more than a cuckoo in the nest anyway.

The more she thought about it, the more she could see Clara's scheming. No doubt, if she thought that her wealthy standing was at risk, it would be in her nature to preserve what was hers.

Ella's bedroom was mostly practical. Her dear father had won the battle with Clara over the wallpaper choice – a stunning green with a rose and ivy leaf pattern. If Clara had had her way, Ella's room would have been whitewashed like the servant's quarters upstairs. The wooden floorboards had been waxed to a gentle sheen by Milly and she had a beautiful Persian rug that was a sage hue.

Her bed was a simple rosewood frame that had a matching style headboard and footboard, with French-style cabriole feet. With matching bedside tables and a writing desk in the corner, everything about her room was functional.

A small dressing table crouched across the corner of her room. It had a small wood-framed mirror in a curved design that sat on top. Ella caught sight of her reflection in the mirror and pushed away from the door. There was no way she could face them down-stairs, judging by the stricken look on her pale face.

The air in her bedroom has grown chilly, and so to give herself something to do, Ella tended to the fire, adding coal from the bucket in the hearth with the brass tongs.

She watched as the embers ignited, mesmerised by the yellow flames licking up around them. Not even the heat that radiated out of the fireplace eased her quivering muscles.

If her father had discovered Thomas's true paternal status, perhaps that had been the source of the many disputes that had wreaked havoc in their home over the years. Or was this a more recent discovery? Her mind spun with the possibilities. Dr Seward had access to all kinds of medication but would a man of his status plot to get rid of her father? Why, after all these years, would he do such a thing?

Ella dusted off her hands and clambered awkwardly to her feet, brushing at her skirts as she did. Her hands caught the package of letters that she had pilfered from her father's office and her heart pitched once more. She'd forgotten all about them.

She pulled them out of the folds of her clothing, reading the writing in the glow from the fire.

Uncle James... He'll help.

An image of her uncle shimmered at the edges of her mind, hazy and blurred through time. Thomas had been barely walking, and her uncle was as gruff as her father was refined. She remembered very little about him, other than her father had said that he was a busy man. Some of the letters looked aged, the envelopes yellowing at the corners. The ink had faded but the twine securing them was new. She couldn't guess why her father had secluded them away at the back of the drawer. Nor why he had kept the news that he was in contact with his brother to himself. It seemed to Ella that almost everything she knew about her family was fast proving to be wrong.

A small open-back chair with a padded seat in the same dark wood as the rest of the furniture was tucked under the writing table. She pulled it out and set the stack of letters amongst the glass bottles of lotion and perfumes. As she sat, she steeled herself against what new findings they would bring. Perhaps she ought to leave them…

The quick knock at the door jolted her. Heart thundering, she quickly stowed the letters in the narrow drawer of her writing desk before she crossed to open the door.

Milly was frowning at the handle as Ella unlocked the door and peered around the edge. "You locked it?"

Ella leaned her head against the wood. The pertinent question was full of concern that was etched into the maid's face. "Sorry." Their friendship was such that Milly would quite often seek sanctuary in Ella's room, even if only for a few minutes. But at this moment, she wasn't sure that she could tolerate even that.

"The bell has gone for supper. I wasn't sure if you'd heard it."

Her stomach boiled at the thought of food. "I'm not feeling well. Would you send my apologies down?"

Milly's brows met. "Is everything alright?"

"I just… I've had a bit of a shock. I'm rather tired."

"Shall I ask Cook for some sandwiches?"

Ella didn't want to talk about any of it right now. She shook her head. "Please, Milly. I just need to be alone."

Before her friend could say another word, Ella shut the door and turned the lock. She wiped her hands nervously down her skirts as she resumed her seat and took out the letters. She undid the knot that her father had made, her heart squeezing to know that he was the last one to have touched these. Pushing away the feelings, she picked up the first letter and began to read.

THE DOOR RATTLED before the timid knock sounded.

Ella lifted her head off the pillow. The fire had died down again, and she could see that dusk had settled. Her stiffness from the chill in the room was a sign of how long she'd lain there lost in thought. The knock sounded again, and she heard Milly calling out softly from the other side of the door.

Putting back her irritation at being disturbed, Ella slid off the bed. She checked that she'd hidden the letters away and that her room looked as it should as she walked to the door. She opened it enough to peer through and her brows met in consternation at the tray Milly held in front of her.

"Milly, please," Ella said grumpily. "I said no–"

"I know," Milly whispered, her eyes sliding back along the empty hall. She cleared her throat and her voice returned to a normal level. "Here is the food you requested, miss."

From her expression, Ella saw that the maid had a reason for disobeying her. "Thank you," she replied, her volume matching Milly's.

She stepped back and Milly rushed in. She set the tray down on the bed and quickly motioned to Ella to shut the door.

"What is it?" Ella hissed.

"I'm sorry, miss!" She murmured. "I know that you said you didn't want to be disturbed but I needed a reason to be up here. Cook was not best pleased to be making an extra plate as it was and gave me a scolding that wasn't much fun."

Ella grabbed a shawl and tossed it over her shoulders, watching the maid carefully. A nervous energy seemed to roll off the young girl and Ella's heart hitched in response. Milly wrung her hands in front of her as she paced.

"Milly! You're going to wear a path doing that. Will you spit out what's troubling you?"

The maid pulled up short, her bottom lip clamped between her teeth. "I'm not sure that I should say anything except..." The pacing resumed. She lifted her hands, letting them fall as she moved. "I'd want to know if it were me. But if I tell, she'll know it must have come from me…"

Ella pressed her fingertips into her temples and rubbed. "Milly, for heaven's sake! Just tell me or don't. I have the most frightful headache, and I don't think I can take any more–"

"They were talking about you!" Milly said quickly, having finally stopped in the middle of the floor.

"Who was?"

"Mrs Tomlinson and the doctor," Milly's eyes dropped to the floor.

Despite the chill in the room, a cold sweat broke out. She tried in vain to keep her voice steady. "What, um, what were they saying?"

The maid's hesitation set Ella's stomach churning. "I may have misheard, or they could have been speaking about someone else."

The events of the day flashed through her mind and somehow, she knew that whatever had been said, she was bound to have been the topic of conversation. Her stepmother needed her out of the house. A cuckoo wasn't welcome in an eagle's nest.

"It's alright, Milly," Ella said gently, trying to ease the distress written on the maid's face. "I won't betray your trust. Tell me what you heard."

"They said you were an encumbrance."

Ella clamped her lips together. It would do them no good for them both to become lost in emotion. "Where was Thomas?"

"He'd been sent to bed. They were in the drawing room. The doctor was enjoying a drop of your father's good brandy, and Mrs Tomlinson was sitting at the fireplace. I doubt they even knew that I was in there. Why would they? A wretch like me is nothing to them."

Ella's shoulders dropped. "I've told you before, this house would be nothing without the staff that runs it."

Milly shook her head, her eyes tracking about the room. They settled on the hearth. "It's cold in here. Let me sort the fire for you."

Ella was about to stop her. Her fingers curled in as the need to shake the rest of the story out of her friend rolled over her, but she understood the need to have something to do whilst her thoughts ran amok.

"Thank you, Milly."

Milly added coal, jabbing at the hearth expertly so that the ashes caught at the coal, and said, "Mrs Tomlinson barely knows my name, miss. But sometimes being invisible comes in handy."

A smile ghosted across Ella's lips, and she lowered herself into her seat, resting her elbow on the dressing table. The headache was clawing at the base of her skull, but she knew that there was more story to come. She waited for Milly to grow still before she prompted her to speak once more.

The maid looked back at her, the orange glow from the fire forming a ring about her. "She called you a millstone to her past. A reminder of Henry for everyone that comes into this house."

Ella believed that she was numb to the insults that

her stepmother could use but it was clear now that Clara was planning on eradicating everything about Henry from this house – including her. Fresh grief pierced her heart, and she folded in on herself, trying to assuage the ache inside.

"The doctor said that they should wait until this summer when your coming out season happens. You'll be of age by then, and it won't seem so shocking. He insisted that they should wait until the time was right but…"

Ella's lifted pained eyes to Milly. "But?"

"Mrs Tomlinson didn't agree with this truth."

A bitter laugh erupted. "I see. So, what does my stepmother have planned for me now?"

"They plan to marry you off to the first man they can find."

CHAPTER 8

"*I*t's not right," Milly muttered. "None of it is. First off, she's marrying before Mr Tomlinson is barely cold in the ground–" Her eyes met Ella's and she grimaced. "Beg pardon, Miss. That was tactless of me. My mother was always telling me to think before I spoke."

Ella's brow flickered. "You're only saying what everyone is probably thinking, Milly."

"Still," her hand fluttered to her throat. "He was a good man, your father. He deserves more."

"He really does," Ella said. They were in the still-room, Ella having sought out her friend for a bit of company lest she went mad from her thoughts going round and round in circles. Nothing had been said to her by either Clara or Dr Seward about getting married, and Ella was hoping that Clara had simply drunk too much wine that night and had been speaking out loud.

Milly pushed the jar full of blackberry jam onto the shelf and held her hand out for the next one. "A widow is meant to be a widow for a year or more, that's the proper way of doing things."

Ella handed her the next item, wondering how the maid would feel if she knew the real reason for Clara marrying so quickly – that Clara was having to move fast to keep a roof over her head and to keep the servants in work. The still-room stores were bare compared to how they'd been just months ago, and it was only a matter of time before Cook or Mrs West had to say something and acknowledge that the coffers were as empty as the cupboards.

Ella didn't want to betray the memory of her father by thinking that he'd left them all in such a state. She closed off her mind from insidious thoughts.

It would be a fate far worse than death for Clara if she were to lose her status and be rendered both home-less and penniless. The doctor was a wealthy man from a decent family. Even without the knowledge that she'd borne his child, it would be a strategic move under any circumstances.

"I dare say my stepmother doesn't care a fig about what the local people say about her," Ella replied.

Milly paused to smirk at Ella, eyes sparkling at the use of such coarse language. The smirk slid to a grin when Ella lifted her chin in challenge. "That's true enough, miss. At least there's been no more mention of you being married off."

"That's true enough. The focus has indeed been on

Thomas, getting him ready for the changes in the school." Ella wished that she could be happier for her brother, but it seemed to her that he could do no wrong. He'd been more cheerful, and it seemed to Ella that he'd simply closed off the part of his heart that had lamented her father. Perhaps he'd known all along that he wasn't Henry's child. It was difficult to live in a house like this when she was surrounded by esoteric secrets.

Milly added the last two jars of quince jelly to the stock and hefted the crate up. "Perhaps they'll wait to match you until after the summer when he's left. By then, you'll be of age."

"Perhaps," Ella hedged.

"You must have a say in whom you marry. Times have moved on."

She thought about her own prospects, about the fact that she wouldn't have a dowry now. No education and no title. She might have to accept whomever they matched her up with if it came to that.

Ella was saved from replying to the question when the door handle rattled briefly before opening inwards, and the cook's head appeared around it.

"There you are, Milly!" She tutted. "What's taking you so long? The bell has just gone for supper." Her eyes lit upon Ella, sitting on the milk stool in the corner. "Oh, beggin' your pardon, Miss Ella," she said, moderating her tone somewhat. "I thought you'd be upstairs readying for your meal."

Ella slowly rose and shook out her long skirts. "I

was just going up," she said mildly. "I helped Milly bring the jars through from the kitchen."

"Right you are, Miss," Cook said, though she sent Milly a dark look full of censorship.

"I offered to help Milly," Ella said quickly to try and save her friend a scolding from the stern woman.

"It's not your place to fetch and carry," Cook admonished. "And Milly not only knows better than that but she's also paid to do these things. Up you go. The bell's been gone more than five minutes and you know how Mrs Tomlinson gets on if she's kept waiting." The cook stood back to allow Ella to pass by. "Oh, and Ella?"

Ella stood along the passageway and looked back. "Hmm?"

"Better make it a good dress. Mrs Tomlinson has the company of Dr Seaward this evening. Her *fiancé*," she added in a dour tone that suggested she was even less impressed with the news than Milly had been.

Ella went via the back stairs. It was narrow and the steps were steep, but it meant that she could bypass the house and move about without being discovered. Clara was never a fan of her associating with the servants but, in truth, Ella felt easier in the company below stairs than she ever had at the fancy dinner parties and soirees when her father and Clara had entertained guests.

She emerged into the empty corridor and swiped at the dusty lint as she scurried down the hall and into her room. She pulled out a navy dress, simple in design and therefore easier for her to get into.

By the time she arrived downstairs, she could hear the murmur of chatter coming from the drawing room. By the volume alone, she could tell that there were more than the usual family members dining that evening.

She slipped through the open door. From how the table had been laid, with fine china and glasses, she knew that her stepmother had put on a show for her guests. The silverware shone from the soft lights in the wall sconces and the chandelier overhead. The fire crackled in the hearth adding to the ambience of comfort and joviality of the guests that turned to look at her.

"There she is!" Clara gushed, beckoning her closer. "We were beginning to think you'd got lost, Ella, my dear."

Looking around the room, Ella didn't recognise a single face that looked back at her. "Forgive me, Clara. I didn't realise that we had company."

The tinkle of laughter and bright smile contrasted with the vice-like grip that encircled her arm. "Now, now, dear. You know I've told you to call me Mother." Ella wasn't given the chance to react as she was pulled closer still and propelled across the carpet by the arm across her back. Clara's voice lowered so that only Ella could hear, "Why did you wear that ghastly dress? These are important people."

She could see Thomas in the corner, deep in conversation with two older men. From the looks of things, no expense had been spared for this occasion. Guests sipped wine and Ella didn't have a clue where it had come from when only last week, there'd been no money to pay the coalman and the shelves were bare. "What's going on?" She whispered back. "Who are these people?"

"Albert's colleagues," Clara murmured, her facsimile smile in place. "Now behave. You show me up and there'll be hell to pay."

"Ella, dear," Dr Seward looked elegantly comfortable in the drawing room where her father had reigned mere months before. Ella tried to keep the anger from her eyes as she joined him. "Come, I want you to meet Mr Marcus Bamford. Marcus, Clara's stepdaughter, Miss Ella Tomlinson."

Manners that had been drilled into her since nursery meant that Ella's smile was as automatic as the hand that she offered to the man who'd not taken his eyes off her since she'd walked into the room.

"Miss Tomlinson." Enigmatically assessing eyes moved down over her form and she wanted to recoil from the stark lust that shone from his face as he bowed slightly. His voice was smooth, and his dark hair had silvered at the temples. "It's a pleasure to make your acquaintance."

Her smile fell as she realised exactly what was going on. She managed to croak out a response, acutely aware of Clara's glare in her periphery. Milly's prediction had been right, after all. Ella looked at Clara, and read the intent in them, even as her heart pounded. They were matchmaking her with this man. They must have been doing it without her knowing and now she'd been ambushed.

"Mr Bowyer works with me at the hospital," Dr Seward informed her convivially, oblivious to her distress as she fought back tears.

"You're a doctor?" Ella asked.

Mocking laughter erupted between the two men and Marcus lifted his cup to toast her. "Forgive us, Miss Tomlinson, but you've stumbled into a long-standing joke. You see, I'm a surgeon. Doctor Seward, here, well... he does the grunt work."

Albert Seward guffawed. "The real work, Marcus. While you pretty boys swoop in for the glory."

Ella didn't understand the rivalry or the thinly veiled comments as they debated the importance of surgery and medicines. She felt cornered, her escape effectively cut off by Clara who was smiling banally at the two men. Ella wondered if the woman even understood what was being said.

She had to bite the inside of her cheek to stop herself from crying as the banter was passed back and forth, each comment containing an element of an undertone where each tried to one-up the other until the gong sounded. The group dutifully took their seats and she saw that the assembly was mostly balanced with men and women, presumably their wives, except for the man who sat next to Thomas... and Marcus Bowyer, who had a vacant seat on his right. Whilst Ella wanted to bolt for the stairs, it seemed Clara had already predicted her response and barred her way.

"We have high hopes for you and Mr Bowyer," she murmured through gritted teeth.

"Do *we* indeed," Ella shot back, their voices obscured as chairs scraped across the polished floor.

"Of course," Clara said. "You're a woman now, Ella. You need to look to your future. And a girl in your position cannot afford to be too choosy."

Ella was about to ask her what that meant but Dr Seward interrupted them, and Ella was left with no choice but to take her seat.

The food was served. Her stomach was a tight knot of anxiety, but she forced herself to chew woodenly. She was aware of Clara and the doctor watching them both, though she refused to meet their looks for fear of what she might see there. Marcus Bowyer was as oily as he looked. She caught his eyes straying below her chin several times and her stomach threatened to heave its contents back onto her plate.

"You've barely eaten enough to feed a bird," Marcus informed her as he wiped the gravy from his chin. The feast consisted of several dishes, including soup, meat, and fish. He had devoured each one. "Are you quite alright?"

She pulled her lips back with a passing smile. She balled up her napkin and set it on the table next to her plate. "Actually, I'm rather tired. If you don't mind, I think I'll retire for the evening."

She pressed her chair back, freezing when his hand

covered hers. He waited until her startled gaze met his. "It was very nice to meet you. I wonder if I might call on you tomorrow."

"I'm flattered, Mr Bowyer. But I'm afraid I–"

"She will love nothing more, Marcus," Clara called across the table.

Ella levelled her stepmother a look. Whatever her plans were here, she wasn't going to be coerced into marrying a stranger. She would marry for love – or a man of her choosing, at least. "I have an appointment tomorrow that I simply can't ignore."

"The day after then," Clara replied smoothly, brooking no argument from the pointed look she was giving Ella. "She will be here at midday, Marcus. Ready and waiting to receive you."

Ella could see just how much effort had gone into the evening, from Clara's perfectly coiffed hair and sparkling adornments to her dress, to the grand feast. They might not be married but it appeared that already Clara was making the most of the doctor's salary. The guests had fallen silent, and Ella was forced to smile, compelled by protocol. She wouldn't bring shame to her father's memory by slinging insults across the table at his widow.

"Thank you, Mr Bowyer. I look forward to seeing you on Tuesday."

Ella was all too aware of the eyes on her back as she retreated from the room. The stairs felt as though she was climbing a mountain and she relied on the sturdy bannisters to leverage her inert body up the staircase.

Her fragile grip on her emotions shattered as soon as the door latched closed behind her.

Soundless sobs twisted inside, her breath leaving her body in gasps. She couldn't marry the obsequious Marcus Bowyer. Her father would have refused to allow such a meeting to occur, let alone spring it on her. Clara was clearing the decks, making way for her son. Ella knew what she had to do. She would write to her uncle and beg him for assistance. She'd do as her father had instructed her to on his deathbed and ask for help.

She was halfway to her writing table when her bedroom door opened inwards. Clara's features were twisted with anger. The door was slammed back into its frame. "How dare you, you ungrateful wretch!"

"What have I done now?"

"Do you realise the situation that Henry left me in? Stuck with two children and not a penny to my name? I'm trying to help you get ahead in life and you turn your back on that help?"

"You're trying to get rid of me," Ella snapped. "To eradicate everything about Henry Tomlinson, including his child. But this is still my father's home!"

Clara's hands balled at her sides, and she advanced on Ella. "It's *my* home now. Your father upped and left me."

Clara swam through the frustrated tears that filled Ella's eyes. "And you seem so utterly heartbroken over this event that you take another man into your bed before my father's body was even cold."

The slap was so quick that Ella didn't have time to register it, let alone move out of the way. Fire exploded in her cheek as she fell against the bed.

"You will marry whom I say, you little witch," Clara leaned closer, venom dripping from every word. "You will do it, or I will scream from the rooftops that your father was a gambler who lost his money. I will ruin his reputation and you'll be in the gutters. Then you can earn your coin on your back when I throw you out onto the streets!"

Ella levered herself off the bed, blood roaring in her ears as her whole body throbbed. Hatred, dark and furious filled her as she glared at Clara. "And I will tell everyone who cares that Thomas isn't a Tomlinson, at all. He's a Seward, and *that* is why you killed my father."

CHAPTER 9

 eth

SETH MILFORD WASN'T sure if it was the gentle knock on his bedroom door or the intrusive click of the door opening that pulled him from his deep slumber.

He was sprawled on the feather-soft mattress on his belly, the covers rumpled across his backside. He listened to the footsteps that moved across the carpeted floor and cracked open one eye to watch Andrew, the footman, place a tray on his sideboard.

The soft grey light filtering around the heavy curtains that covered the long bedroom window told him that it was still early, and he remembered that he was at his father's country estate. The tantalising scent of coffee that reached him was probably an act of contrition from his mother. Throughout the dull headache squeezing his cranium was latent anger, left-over from the blazing argument he'd had with his father the night before.

On the bedside table, a silver tray held a decanter of brandy and a single crystal glass, reminding him of the reason for his headache. Not even the fine quality spirit could eradicate the disaster of an evening from his memory.

"Andrew," Seth rasped, "I said to Mr Dwyer that I wouldn't need a wake-up call today."

The footman was setting out his day clothes and, without looking back, he said, "The instruction came from Mrs Milford. She said, and I am quoting here, sir, you are not permitted to sulk today of all days. Drink the coffee and come down for breakfast."

Seth roused himself enough onto his elbows so he could scrub at his face. He blinked groggily at the young man, having to tamp down on the spurt of annoyance. After all, it was not Andrew's fault that he had an interfering mother hellbent on seeing her first-born married to a suitable match, simply so she could tick off two out of the three children.

"I'm assuming Ophelia and her father are still here?"

"I believe they are, yes, though they have not yet got up, if that helps, sir."

Seth sighed heavily and pushed back the coverlet, so he could swing his legs free. Uncaring of his nakedness, he held his hands out for his gown.

"Will that be all, sir?" Andrew asked.

Seth cinched the belt of the rope around his waist,

"Are you happy Andrew?"

The question took the young man by surprise. "Sir?"

Seth poured himself a coffee, adding a splash of milk and a cube of sugar to the cup, looking up as he stirred the beverage. "I'm asking you if you're happy in your life right now. Speak frankly, please."

The young lad blinked at him, visibly uncomfortable. "My father worked all his life in a filthy mine," he admitted reluctantly. "He died, coughing up black muck and fighting for every breath. My mum brags to her neighbours that I have a job in such a fine house. If I'm to speak frankly, sir?"

"Whatever you say won't go beyond these four walls," Seth assured him.

Andrew gave a nod. "A few more shillings at the end of the week wouldn't go a miss," he said, drawing back the curtains now that Seth was decent. "But I'm happy, sir. I have my eye on one of the maids here. I would like to make a butler, one day. Maybe open a little hotel on the coast to run in my retirement." A small wistful smile pulled at the footman's lips.

Seth settled a hand on Andrew's shoulder and squeezed him reassuringly. "That's a fine dream for a bright young lad like yourself."

Andrew thanked Seth and left the room, and Seth leaned against the window, his eyes tracking the familiar rolling lines of the gardens, the fields, and the small village beyond their lands.

Although Seth wouldn't admit it out loud, he envied the young man for his freedom. Seth was worldly enough to know that he lived a privileged life. It afforded him many experiences that wealth allowed. He read enough newspapers and articles to know that not all that glittered was gold in their fair city.

His father had acquired a fleet of ships, seeing the need for faster and stronger ships. Philip had been amongst the first to buy iron-hulled boats from Belfast, and their wealth accumulated when the steam engines grew faster and bigger.

Seth knew that he had a life that many would envy, and the business side of things excited him. As a very wealthy young man, Seth often found himself the target of hopeful mothers and their fortune-seeking daughters hoping to catch his eye. He found the whole process bothersome, but his good manners meant that he had to use fancy words to let these women down gently. He'd been perfectly content with his life; spending his mornings at the docks, observing the comings and goings of the boats, negotiating with the captains of the many ships in his father's fleet, as well as ensuring that cargo was dealt with, and payments were met. He did not need a wife.

He wasn't sure why his parents were so fanatical about changing this fact. They had Giles, his younger brother, to marry off, although Giles was certainly the playboy of the family. He contributed nothing to the wealth that he spent so frivolously.

Prudence had her fancy American husband and no doubt there would soon be grandchildren to occupy his mother.

But he'd felt blindsided last night. And Ophelia was most certainly keen. She'd bored him stupid with her insipid observations of Parisian fashions and her friends being courted. The evening had dragged by until they'd split; men to enjoy cigars and the women to…well, whatever it was that women did in the parlour. Nothing that he'd care to hear, of that he was certain.

The fact that his mother and father had already begun to plan the wedding that he knew nothing of had ignited his fury. As soon as Denis had left the room, Seth had exploded.

Seth dressed quickly and made his way down the stairs. He found his mother in the parlour, exquisitely presented and with hair perfectly styled.

"Good morning, Mama," he intoned dutifully as he took his seat.

She eyed him keenly like a dressmaker looking for an errant stitch. "Why do you look so tired, Seth? I need you to be your best today."

Biting back on his initial caustic retort, he busied his hands with making a second cup of coffee. "Seeing as I'm returning to London shortly, I hardly think my shoddy appearance would be cause for concern."

Her cup clattered back into its saucer as she looked at him, aghast. "You are most certainly *not* going back to London today, Seth. We have guests," she leaned forward, her lips barely moving through the whisper, "Guests here to see you, I might add."

"They aren't here at my request though, are they?

Though I'm sure Father has already apprised you of our little conversation after dinner last night."

Judging from her pinched expression, he could see that she'd been apprised of the blazing argument and more. She straightened up, staring out of the picturesque bay window. "You are twenty-seven years old, Seth. That's more than time enough. Your father needs to secure the future of the company, and you are duty-bound to comply."

"Mother, please save the dramatics for your women's circle," Seth sighed. "You make it sound as if the fate of a country rests on my shoulders. I am sick to the back teeth of your interfering. I love you both dearly and am entirely grateful for the opportunities that the company has afforded me–"

"Exactly!" Sarah crowed triumphantly. "You must show your gratitude by marrying. Ophelia and her father are a good match for you. Not quite the match I'd made with Lavinia–"

"One would think you'd have learned your lesson by now then, Mama. I was completely blindsided last night when that girl started talking about weddings to me. It was humiliating," he added fiercely as renewed shame washed over him. "Not even the courtesy of a letter to warn me that we had company, let alone that you'd already been in talks with the girl's mother."

"You wouldn't have come here if I'd have written, Seth," Sarah said resignedly. "Why do you hate me so?"

Seth dug his finger and thumb into his eye sockets, wishing for the patience to deal with his mother and the hangover together. "Mother, please." When his hand fell away, Sarah was looking at him tearfully. "I know that you're disappointed in me, but you have Prudence already safely attached. You still have Giles to go. There's time yet for me, Mama."

"Not always, Seth. That's the only commodity we can never make more of."

His brow furrowed as he searched her face. The brackets at the sides of her mouth seemed deeper, her eyes were shadowed, and even the lines around her eyes were more pronounced. His heart jolted as a dark thought slithered into his mind. "That's a strange thing to say," he said softly. "Mama, are you quite well?"

Her hesitation turned the coffee in his stomach to acid. Her smile was slight and fleeting. "I'm fine, Seth. A little piqued, perhaps."

He scanned her expression for more details as if that could shake the truth from her, but it wasn't appropriate for him to ask her any further questions as Dwyer announced Ophelia and her father.

"Good morning, Denis," Seth took over the duties of the host to allow his mother a little time to recover.

He put aside his concern for her health, making a mental note to ask the butler if the doctor had made any house calls here recently. His mother might drive him to distraction most days, but he wasn't a monster. The thought of losing a parent left him feeling a little morose.

"Good morning." The older man took his seat. His daughter swept in behind him. He remembered from his conversation with her last night that she'd brought her lady's maid with her as no one else knew how to style her hair. She wore a lovely rose-coloured silk dress that suited her cool complexion.

"I trust you both slept well?" Seth asked once they were seated and had food in front of them.

"It's terribly quiet here," Ophelia said.

"I, for one, enjoy the tranquillity," Denis stated.

"You ought to come for the shooting season," Sarah said. "Philip simply adores August for the grouse and pheasants."

"Do you shoot, Seth?" Denis asked him.

"I do," Seth replied.

"I'm afraid it turns into quite the contest between the boys," Sarah said with more than a hint of pride.

"But there's nothing for miles," Ophelia said. "I'm sure I'd tire of this place soon enough. Where is your townhouse that Papa mentioned, Seth?"

"It's in Regent's Park."

"A friend has just acquired the most delightful, terraced house in Baker Street," Ophelia told him. "All modern furnishings. None of these dour oil paintings that the older generation insist upon," she waved around the room at the various art.

"You're not a fan of art?"

Ophelia sniffed daintily. "I think that it has its place, just not in the home I plan to have."

"There is a painting named 'Ophelia,'" Seth said. "By the artist John Millais."

83

As expected, the girl preened. "I didn't know that. Is it very beautiful?"

"It is, indeed. It's a stunning oil by a talented artist trying to capture the beauty in something emotive," Seth replied, ignoring the warning look from his mother. "It depicts the scene in Hamlet where Ophelia drowns herself."

Sarah's shrill laughter filled the shocked silence. "Goodness, Seth, it's breakfast time!"

Seth dabbed at the corners of his mouth with his napkin and pushed his chair back from the table. He pretended not to notice the twin looks of horror and disappointment on the women's faces. "If you'll excuse me?"

"You're not leaving, are you?"

It was his mother's sharp tone that curdled his stomach. "No, Mama. I have some correspondence that I must attend," he paused, feeling a little of the dread over his mother's health push through his irritation with Ophelia. Why his mother thought that they'd be a good match was beyond him. "I should like to take a walk in the gardens shortly. Ophelia, would you care to join me? With your supervision, of course, Mr Harrison."

With an agreement in place, he returned to his bed chamber. He decided that he would dance to his mother's tune to appease her just this once. He would speak with the young woman and then let her know gently but with finality, that there was no future in any dalliance that she was planning with him.

CHAPTER 10

 lla

EVEN BEFORE THE lock turned in the door, Ella knew that she'd made a grave mistake revealing her hand to Clara. Her secret was out, and Clara no longer had to pretend to be acting in Ella's best interests. Still, Ella's only hope was that Clara's need to maintain status outweighed her desire to ruin her stepdaughter.

Ella rolled onto her knees, her body protesting at the movement. She ached along her ribs and her lip throbbed as if it had a pulse. Her breath hissed between her gritted teeth as she stood up and crept over to the jug and bowl in the corner of her room. She avoided the mirror, not wanting to see the damage that Clara's furious attack had inflicted on her face. She didn't need to see it; the stinging as she gingerly dabbed the cloth to her face was telling enough, and the bowl in the water turned red as she wrung out the cloth. The only consolation that she could take from what had just happened was the knowledge that Clara wouldn't permit her to see the unctuous Marcus Bowyer until her face had healed.

After she'd cleaned her face, she slowly removed the remainder of the pins that she'd secured her dark hair with. Without bothering to brush it out, Ella returned to her bed and curled into a ball, uncaring of the ruined dress.

Her father had often warned her that her tendency to speak rashly would get her in trouble and now it seemed that his dire predictions had come true at the worst time. But she'd been unable to help the flare of temper, or the desire to strike at Clara, even though her stepmother was ten steps ahead of her in the plans to scrub any existence of her father from his house.

Salt from her tears stung the cuts on her face but she let them fall unchecked. Perhaps her impetuous nature was deserving of this fate. She longed for the comfort of her father's arms, for the protection that he'd always provided for her. She cried for the loss of her saviour even as she longed to rail at him for the poor decisions that he'd made that left them all destitute.

Long after the fire had turned to cold ash, she lay there as possibilities rolled through her mind. The sky rolled from pitch black, the grey light edging around the heavy curtains over the long sash window. Hollow-eyed, she cautiously moved off the bed and across to her writing desk. She'd put off writing to her Uncle James but now she was left with no choice. She could only hope to throw herself upon his mercy and beg for help. From the tone of the letters she'd read, she knew that tensions were still high between the brothers. From an outsider looking in, Ella surmised that each was as stubborn as the other and unwilling to admit defeat. Perhaps the demise of his older brother would mean that their rift was in part forgiven.

Ella scribbled quickly, giving a brief explanation of what had happened. She left out the part where she believed her father's death had been too convenient. She had no proof, and it wouldn't serve her well to cast such aspersions on Dr Seward without any. Instead, she simply asked her uncle to fulfil her father's dying wish – that he helps her.

She sealed the envelope and tucked it away. When the maid came to tend to the fire, she would slip her the envelope and beg her to post it. But the morning rolled on with no sign of Milly or any other servant. She had no fuel for the fire in her room and the only source of water was in the blood-stained bowl. Ella heard the occasional footfall beyond the confines of her room. More than once, she resorted to banging futilely against her bedroom door. Yet the day rolled past midday.

Although she had no appetite, her head was pounding, and she desperately wanted a drink of water. Her fury dissolved into despair; Clara was reminding her just how much control she had over Ella's destiny. It wouldn't matter if her uncle was willing to help her if she couldn't reach him.

The shadows had lengthened in the room as evening approached when the key was finally slid into her bedroom lock.

Ella sprung to her feet, though her initial spurt of relief at seeing Milly's familiar form bearing a laden tray was short-lived when she saw Clara behind her. There was no way of slipping the letter concealed in her dress to Milly whilst Clara was there. She'd have to wait for another time. Milly's horrified expression when she saw Ella's damaged face conveyed just how bad she must look. But the maid was well-trained and carried the tray past Ella without a word.

"I'll fetch you some wood, miss," she said quietly.

"You'll do no such thing," Clara said from behind her. "Ella has enough clothing in here to keep warm. She'll put some of them on if needed, won't you?" Ella remained mute as Milly's brows rose and her step hesitated, then she changed direction and instead reached for the chamber pot. "You can leave that, too."

"But it needs–"

"You will remember your position in this house, girl. Now, you can go back to cleaning. The salon is a pigsty."

"Yes, miss." Milly scurried out of the bedroom.

Ella wanted to defend Milly. She was many things in this house – chambermaid, housemaid and scullery maid – but she worked endlessly and kept the rooms spotless. But Ella was wary of igniting Clara's wrath anymore and so kept quiet. A strained silence filled the room.

"You'll eat."

It was a statement, not a suggestion. Ella's body tensed with fear, and she kept her gaze downcast.

"Do you hear me?"

Ella nodded once.

"I've rearranged your appointment with Marcus. I couldn't have you showing me up looking like... well, that," Clara said unkindly. "I explained that you're sick. I have warned him about your sickness, that you get confused at times."

Ella imagined the lies that Clara was spinning to the servants on why she'd been locked in here. Her jaw ached from gritting her teeth.

"You'll eat and recover. Albert is already making the arrangements."

Ella's gaze snapped up then. "What arrangements?"

Clara's lips peeled back as her hand rested on the door handle. Panic seized Ella when Clara moved to close the door.

"Clara, what arrangements?"

"Why, your wedding, of course."

Ella's jaw dropped open. "And just whom am I supposed to marry?"

ANNIE SHIELDS

"Marcus Bowyer," she stated as if that should have been abundantly clear already.

Ella shook her head. "Don't be absurd. I barely know him."

Scorn glinted in her eyes. "Don't you dare speak to me like that, Ella! Don't you *dare*! You are already on very thin ice in this house after your outrageous lies about me last night."

Ella clamped her lips shut, refusing to defend her claims. She'd have to admit to eavesdropping on the couple, for a start, and she didn't want another beating.

Victory shone on Clara's face. She pulled her chin back, a smirk flirting with her thin lips. "If you haven't noticed by now, I am in control. You will marry him, and you will go quietly from this house to his. I will have fulfilled any obligation denoted by society and I'll finally be rid of you."

"I will not go!" Ella fired back. "You cannot make me marry someone I don't know. Times have changed! I will refuse in the church, and I will–"

"You will go, or I'll see to it that Albert has you sent to the asylum. He has the power, you know. Poor Henry Tomlinson's daughter, driven quite mad by grief. She was sent there to prevent herself from doing any more harm. I've already told Milly what I caught you doing last night," she pointed to Ella's bruised and battered face.

"*You* did this to me!" Shock, twinned with terror, rolled through her and her voice turned desperate. The asylum hospitals were frightening places, but she knew that a man like Dr Seward would certainly have the power to carry out her threats. "Clara, please!"

Clara shook her head as she stepped back into the doorway, pulling the door with her. "No one will believe you, Ella. So, I'll leave the choice to you. Eat and make yourself strong for marriage to Marcus or starve and face the lunatic asylum."

The door slammed shut. Ella rushed at it, screaming for her stepmother to return as she pounded ineffectively against the surface. But no one came to save her. As her fight ebbed away, she lowered her forehead to the door. Perhaps she had no more tears to cry. The hallway beyond her prison was silent and Ella realised that she was trapped. Clara was beyond reason. She knew that Milly and Ella were friends – why else would she have accompanied Milly? Her only chance of escape had been closed off. Ella leaned back against the door and slid down until her rump met the floor.

Long after nightfall had descended, Ella crawled over the floor, feeling her way to the bedside table. She found the candlestick and lit it, the soft glow sizzling as the flame danced. The choices laid out to her were clear. Marry a stranger whom would no doubt be made to think that Ella was a danger to herself or else be locked away from society.

But a third option had occurred to her in the gloom.

Resolutely, she opened her drawers and began to add her belongings to a roughly made cloth bag. Her suitcases and trunks were in the attic so she couldn't access them, not that she'd be able to carry them all with her anyway. She wouldn't be able to travel anywhere without any money when she was only on foot. So, she'd take just what she needed.

Then she began to eat. And she'd wait for the right moment to run.

CHAPTER 11

 eth

"How did things go with Ophelia, old chap?" William asked.

His new brother-in-law was a pleasant enough fellow. His pallid aspect and timid manner meant that he was often overlooked by men, though Seth knew that William had a shrewd mind for business. His healthy bank balance made him an attractive prospect for Sarah Milford's only daughter, even if Prudence had complained about William's dreary countenance and thinning hair after their first introduction. Unlike her brothers, Prudence was obedient and complied with the instruction from her parents that William was to be the man for her.

Before Seth could respond, Prudence answered her

husband's question on his behalf, "They looked incredibly cosy from where Mama and I were watching them."

"Your mother said that you were walking the gardens for quite some time. Can we assume that you've changed your mind after last night's tantrum?"

Seth took his time replying to his father, sipping from the wine cup. The long mahogany dining table was occupied by the family at one end, with the ornately carved chairs that flanked it mostly empty after last night's gathering. The silver cutlery reflected the soft glow from the glowing chandelier overhead. The walls were hung with oil paintings of landscapes and ancestors. He set his glass down and cleared his throat, trying to find the best way to tell his parents that he'd sent the silly girl away home disappointed and annoyed with him.

"Ophelia will make a fine wife for someone, I'm sure of it. But," he looked pointedly around the table at his parents and his siblings, "that someone will not be me."

"Do you have any idea how much work went into that matchmaking?" Philip ground out, his face growing darker with each syllable.

"I will say this to you all so that there is no uncertainty," Seth enunciated. "If I have to marry, it will be at my choosing."

"You are twenty-seven years of age," his father told him. "By your age, your mother had borne me three children. I was well on the way to my fifth boat."

Seth sighed in exasperation. "We've been through this before, Papa. And it's getting quite tiresome having to repeat myself."

"None of us are getting any younger, Seth," Phillip said. "I want to meet my grandchildren before I die."

"Seth, you didn't even give the girl a chance."

It was Sarah's simple sentence that spiked him with guilt. "I did as you asked. I walked around with the girl for more than an hour. She spoke of nothing more than what can only be described as drivel. I tuned out after listening to her prattle on about a dress for a full ten minutes. She has no opinion on politics or the vote. How can I build a life with a woman who is as uninspired as she?"

"You can grow to love someone, dear," Sarah petted her husband inanely. "Meet with her again. See if you can find room in your heart for her."

"It's like a flower," Prudence supplied helpfully. "It needs to be fed and nurtured, right, Mama?"

"Please, Seth. Don't refuse her just yet."

Seth searched his mother's face, wondering if this need of hers to match her children was due to the illness that she'd hinted at, or because she had nothing better to do with her time.

"Times are changing. I'm certain that a man as connected as Denis Harrison would be a useful contact for us," Seth hedged.

"He's stinking rich, Seth. That will tide the company over for years to come. Who cares what interests the girl?" Philip harumphed. "This is a dynasty for your children."

"I shall make my return to London this evening," Seth said, sidestepping the question, and trying to avoid another confrontation with his father. "We have much work to do with several shipments pending."

"Shipments that could well use the docks and storage in the warehouses that Harrison had. It was a perfect match, combining the two houses," Philip stated as if it should've been obvious to his son. "She is a handsome girl, what more could you want?"

Seth slapped his hand down on the table so that the plates rattled, and his mother yelped. "Just because a convenience match made sense for you and Mama, doesn't mean that all matches will be successful. And as frivolous as it may sound to a businessman like yourself, Father, if I ever marry then I wish to marry for love."

Giles sniggered in the corner. Seth turned his glare on his youngest sibling. "I really don't think you're in any position to laugh, dear brother. One day, after you finished catting it all around Edinburgh city, you'll have to come into the business and learn everything, just as I have done."

Giles shook his head and held up his hands in surrender. "Not me," he replied. "My career lies in engineering."

"Over my dead body!" Philip roared. "No son of mine will waste his life after my ancestors have shed blood, sweat & tears to give you this business!"

As the rumbling disagreements grew between Giles and his father, Sarah leaned forward, laying a hand on Seth's forearm.

"She's an attractive prospect, Seth. From a good family. Can't you find it in your heart to at least try?"

"Mama, please," Seth began.

Sarah sensed his wavering like a bloodhound and pressed on, her voice low. "I thought your father to be an overbearing brute when I was introduced to him."

Seth's lips twitched, his gaze moving past his mother's earnest expression to the puce-coloured face of an irate Philip as he argued with Giles. An overbearing brute suited him.

"Mama, for once, I'd like to meet a woman who's not looking to secure a foothold financially."

Sarah cupped a hand around his cheek. "Spoken with the naivety of youth, my boy. But for our kind, we must think of our future as a family. Our financial status makes you a target for fortune hunters, but Ophelia has an income of her own. She would be a good match for you…if you just gave her a chance."

Seth's gaze dropped to his plate, the pressure of his mother's stare eroding his appetite. Several of his friends were courting or already married. He knew that he had a duty to carry on the bloodline – he just always envisioned it being at his own pace, to a woman whom he admired, not someone as characterless as Ophelia. Swallowing his pride and years of dreaming about finding a woman who inspired him, he said, "Fine."

CHAPTER 12

lla

It was as though Clara knew that Ella was waiting for an opportunity to run. The bedroom door was only opened once or twice a day, and Clara was always present when the tray arrived. She seemed to derive pleasure by reminding Ella just how little control she had over her own life.

Once the swelling had reduced, and the bruising had faded, the one time she'd been allowed out of her room was when Clara played chaperone to Marcus for afternoon tea. Ella stumbled through the charade; her nerves stretched to breaking point as she was forced to converse with the old man. She smiled and nodded, trying to show willingness if only to counter any stories that Clara chose to make up about her.

Not even bathing was off-limits to Clara's company. Her stepmother stood behind the screen, explaining her plans for Ella's wedding that were now fixed for the following month.

If Ella had ever had any grandiose ideas of falling in love the way her father had fallen in love with her mother, she was quickly disillusioned as to the options that were left for her. More than once, Ella had contemplated climbing through her bedroom window, but the sharp drop would surely kill her. However, Clara put paid to any crazy ideas by nailing the sash window shut.

Ella dressed herself, the warm spring sunshine beyond the window almost mocking her. She guessed that it must be Sunday by the people walking along the road in the smart house coats and hats who were going to church.

Ella heard the key in the lock and prepared herself for the daily battle, but her mouth dropped open in surprise when it was Cook that filled the doorway instead of Milly and Clara.

The other woman had swapped her grey uniform and dusty white apron for a smarter-looking dark navy dress. Her snowy white hair was curled up under a purple felt hat, held in place with a pearl and garnet pin.

"Cook?"

"Yes, yes," Cook waved her forward, the action as short as her tone. "Quickly. Everyone is at church. Let's go before you are seen." The keys dangling from the lock rattled as she pushed the door wider and showed Ella her coat. She must have taken it from the coat stand in the hallway. "Don't just gawp at me, girl! Or do you want to marry that dreadful man?"

Ella didn't need to be asked twice. She dropped to her knees and reached under her bed, tugging free the small cloth bag that she'd packed weeks ago. She scrambled back to her feet and darted to her writing table where she grabbed the pack of her uncle's letters from the top drawer.

"She'll know it's you," Ella said breathlessly as she followed the stout woman along the hall and down the stairs. "You'll lose your job."

"She won't," Cook scoffed, leaning heavily on the thin rail as she hobbled down the stairs. "She's got Milly glued to her because she suspects that the poor girl is in cahoots with you. God knows we've tried all sorts of excuses for her to allow Milly up the stairs, if only to speak with you unencumbered, but that woman…" She caught herself and walked down a few more treads.

"She's clever," Ella admitted. She'd underestimated Clara at every turn. She'd spent hour after hour going over her past and she realised just how much Clara had manipulated everyone.

"Devious," Cook agreed. "I told Clara that I wanted some time away. They all think I'm visiting my ailing sister for a few days," she sent a quick grin over her shoulder. "I don't have a sister. No one knows I'm here, not even Milly, so at least the poor girl cannot be

accused of anything. The keys were left in the office –
Milly told me where they were kept – so I decided to
sneak back in when I knew the house would be empty."

Ella was stunned into stopping. "You've done all
that for me?"

Cook stopped on the stairs, frowning at Ella's feet.
"Don't dilly-dally now, else it'll all be for nowt.
Come on!"

Ella began again, her heart racing.

She waited in the hallway long enough for Cook to
return the key to its spot and then they set off for the
back stairs. Walking through the home, Ella could see
now what all the noise she'd been hearing in the past
few weeks was. Furniture that she didn't recognise
gleamed in the rooms that they passed, new carpet and
curtains complemented the garish ornaments on
display. Clara's plans for removing every speck of
Tomlinson from the house were in full swing. Ella
could only assume that Albert Seward was indulging
his fiancée as much as Henry Tomlinson had.

She'd been cooped up for so long that it felt very
strange being back below stairs. She hurried along the
passageway behind the puffing cook toward the back
door. The cook dipped for a small case at the door and
held it out to Ella.

"It's not much, granted, but it's less conspicuous
than what's in your hand now."

Ella stared at the case, knowing that these things
held value, even in the battered state it was. "Please,
you've already done so much for me. I have no way of

repaying you for your kindness, but I can't take that from you."

Cook rolled her eyes impatiently. "Take it. It will draw less attention than a bed sheet tied into a knot. You're a young woman looking for work, not a hobo drifting. Do you have a plan? Milly seemed to think that you had a place in mind."

"Yes, my u–"

The cook cut her off, leaning away as she flapped her hand. "I don't want to know. That way, I won't have to lie when I am asked. Here," she reached into her pocket and handed her a leather pouch. "It's not much but it'll get you started."

The pouch jingled as it was passed to her. Even from just the weight, Ella could tell that there were many coins inside. "No, I can't take this."

The cook pressed her hand back, expression resolute. "You can and you will. Henry Tomlinson saw to it that my father had work when he was injured. He gave my mother a glowing reference so that she was able to feed all of us bairns. Your mother took me on as a maid without a scrap of experience, Ella. This is the least I can do for them." Ella's throat worked as a wave of emotion crashed over her and the cook's face softened. "If he did run the accounts down as she says, it's because she emptied them and gave him no choice but to take a gamble. She might be pretty to look at, but she's got a black heart. Far too often, she has interfered in my kitchen, adding to my menu when no one knew your father's tastes better than I did. I'll be beggared if she will tarnish his good name and ruin your life in the process."

Ella bit the inside of her cheek, managing a small nod, her tears scalding her eyes. "Thank you."

They slipped out of the back door, Ella's heart pounding with terror. Her breath puffed in tight gasps as she walked alongside Cook, her body screaming with awareness as she strained to hear Clara's shrill voice demanding that she return to her prison, or footsteps to signal they were being followed. Even the crunch of wheels on the road made her whirl in panic but Cook urged her along the pavement.

"Where are we going?" Ella asked as they arrived at the omnibus stop.

"You can stay the night with me. I have lodgings for the night. A decent meal and a good night's sleep, then I'll return here, and you'll go to… wherever it is you're going."

The stumbling of words spoke volumes. Cook suspected exactly where Ella was heading. She worried that her disappearance would have ramifications for the staff who'd been a part of her life for so long.

"You can't think about that now," the cook said gently when Ella spoke out loud. "We're all old enough and ugly enough to take care of ourselves."

"Not Milly." The thought of leaving her friend behind filled her with dread. Milly had been like a sister to her, and she wouldn't be able to say goodbye to her.

Cook assisted Ella up the steps of the omnibus,

slapping away the wandering hand of the driver. She paid their fares and took up a seat. The faces of the passengers were distorted as Ella gave in to her tears. Fear chilled her as she was faced with a different kind of uncertainty. How could she even hope to survive in a city when she'd been coddled in the arms of her father her whole life?

She was leaving behind everything that she knew. She could only hope that her uncle would give her shelter.

CHAPTER 13

 eth

"If Gladstone has his way, they'll be letting every Tom, Dick and Harry vote before we know it."

Seth allowed the wine to swirl around his mouth, hiding his mirth at the statement. A glance across the table at their host Mr Abernathy spoke volumes. Abernathy was keen to keep up appearances and it was obvious that the meal had cost a pretty penny. Seth had also been good friends with his son, Peter, for many years. They'd formed a friendship of four during their stint at Eton – comprising Seth, Peter, Cuthbert, and Freddie Walton – whom was the only one of them missing this evening.

Mr Abernathy was an engineer who'd honed his skills as an ironmonger and brass founder apprentice during his years in Bath. Abernathy had broken away from the company when a clause in his apprenticeship agreement had forbidden him to marry until the apprenticeship was complete. There was nothing that the man couldn't make in metal, nor an engineering problem that he couldn't solve, which had meant that he'd been able to secure work, building his business successfully.

Abernathy had the Midas touch until one of his apprentices had been killed in his workshop. He'd weathered the negative press and the dip in trade, but the death of his daughter had impacted Abernathy's brilliance. He'd been making grounds for repairing his reputation when a fire last year had devastated his business. Peter had spoken often about his father's apparent run of bad luck and had come to Seth for advice, so Seth knew that the foundry they owned was in trouble. But the talk had taken a turn toward politics. Seth knew from experience that political stances could make or break a business deal, and Abernathy's foundry needed an injection of cash soon.

The seating pattern was balanced enough, and Seth found himself sitting between Peter's sister, Lydia, and Cuthbert Wilson's fiancée, Jane Gilbert, a clever woman with bright green eyes and fiery-red hair.

"Let's hope so," Jane commented to the room. "I, for one, think that it's a move in the right direction. Why shouldn't those men have a say? They work the land, and I say it can only be a good thing. It will give a balanced view."

Cuthbert, his face already glowing from his wine consumption, scoffed, "Jane, dear, I don't think we need to hear unhelpful input."

John Wilson, Cuthbert's father, snorted. "Hear, hear, son. A woman has no place in politics."

Jane's mouth pinched at the edges. "You don't think that women deserve the vote, too, Mr Wilson?"

"No, I most certainly do not. Who would run the home if we allowed them to meddle in things they don't understand?"

The table fell silent, and Seth could feel resentment rolling off his table companion. But Jane remained quiet, making a show of returning to her meal, although Seth noticed that nothing passed her lips.

The dining hall was illuminated in the soft glow of gas lamps and candles, a testament to Abernathy's mistrust of modern conveniences. Or perhaps it was to hide the faded gold and cream wallpaper that curled in the edges. The table was set with the finest of silverware and crystal, though the table was missing fresh flowers. It was these little elements that lent an air of overcompensation for a dinner party.

"I'm still uncertain how Gladstone managed to win the seat back," John Wilson said to the room at large.

"He's a dynamo," another commented. "I was at school with his son. He told me that his father devours reading material like it's going out of fashion. That he will compose a fifteen-thousand essay on Tennyson before breakfast."

"His views will plunge us into war," John Wilson muttered.

Seth caught Peter's pleading look. With a slight nod, he asked, "Mr Abernathy, did your delivery reach New York?"

Abernathy chewed and dabbed at his mouth before he replied, "It did. I'm told they're most impressed with the engineering."

John Wilson cocked a brow. "A delivery?"

"That's right," Seth said. "Mr Abernathy, you'll have to forgive my ignorance. Perhaps you could explain to Mr Wilson what it was?"

"It seems that there's a man by the name of Trivett who'd starting a mineral water business in North America. He needed a bottle-making machine to put the gas into the liquid and seal it. He prefers English machinery," Abernathy said. "Seth was good enough to arrange shipment via a barge to Bristol before it was taken to New York."

"Is there much demand for this type of work?"

"Indeed," Mr Abernathy replied. "Infusing water with carbon dioxide isn't a new concept but with demand climbing, there is a need to make the process more efficient. I'm told that people add flavours to the liquids, too."

John Wilson had a nose for investment. He speared up a piece of meat with his fork and before it was put in his mouth, he muttered, "I do agree that English machinery is the finest in the world. Perhaps we ought to talk later over a brandy."

Abernathy's shoulders almost slumped with his relief. "I have some cigars that I think you might like."

"Now that I can get on board with," John Wilson said with a laugh.

The conversation moved on and Seth hoped that Mr Abernathy could close on the deal.

"Bravo, Mr Milford," Jane murmured next to him. "That was well steered."

Seth smiled at her. "One does what one can to help a friend."

"I imagine your father will miss your negotiation skills once you're in America."

"Pardon?"

Jane met his puzzled gaze with a furrowed brow. "Cuthbert tells me you're marrying an American, and that you'll be needed over there to oversee the many properties."

Seth aimed a dark look across the table at his friend, who was unaware of the attention as he guffawed loudly at something his father had just said.

"I heard the same," Lydia leaned in from the other side. "It was the talk of the dinner I was at last week, about how someone has finally managed to snag your attention, Seth. I met the young lady around Christmas. She's very attractive though, I must say, I wasn't sure I believed it when everyone knows that you're a sworn bachelor."

Seth rolled his lips, even as his annoyance tipped over into anger. "I've met her once."

"Yes," Lydia breathed, lashes fluttering dreamily, "It

made quite the story, how your gazes connected across the crowded room."

Usually, the gossip around town rarely bothered him. After all, it was usually perpetuated by bored young women who had nothing more to do with their time. With the Milford fortune behind him, he was used to being the object of speculation. Still, he couldn't say with any degree of certainty if this rumour hadn't been started from within his own household. Sarah was like a dog with a bone, tenacious and dedicated.

"I'm afraid you've been most misinformed, ladies."

"Really?" Lydia asked doubtfully. "I was led to believe that it was a done deal. Ophelia Harrison was seen at House of Worth in Paris just last week. One can only assume it was to discuss wedding dress designs."

Seth regretted agreeing with his mother to meet again with Ophelia and knew that it was going to take more than some fancy words to extricate himself from this tangle of rumours.

CHAPTER 14

lla

ELLA COULD TELL that she was getting closer to the Docklands.

It wasn't just the skyline that she could see that was peppered with the spikes of ship masts, gathered closer together in a thicket, but also the smell of salt water and fish that mingled with the stench of sewage and coal smoke.

The streets were narrow and crowded, filled with people of all colours and creeds bustling together. Sailors, dockworkers, and merchants mingled with the passengers that flocked off the ships. The clothing of each marked their purpose, ranging from satin waistcoats to oiled leather trousers or the customs-house officer and his brass button jacket. Women, their low-cut dresses revealing a different type of trade altogether, strolled amongst the crowds, there to seek a coin from the stream of men who'd been at sea for months.

Warehouses and factories lined the wharves, their walls stained with soot and grime. The steely sky was disrupted by tall chimneys, belching black clouds of acrid smoke.

The docks themselves were a maze of piers, canals, and locks, all teeming with ships of every shape and size. Steamships hissed and burped smoke as their cargo was unloaded, while barges and narrowboats darted in and out of waterways like rats.

The stench from the river was contrasted with smells of coffee and spices, or rum and tobacco, depending on which way the wind blew.

The clanging of metal and the creaking of wooden carts was a constant backdrop, punctuated with the bellows of captains who cupped their hands around their mouths as they screamed at the sailors under their command.

Ella tried not to stare at the various sights and sounds that assaulted her senses. The cobblestone roads were darkened from the damp air that pressed in on her.

She'd risen at first light and had choked down the breakfast served her by the grouchy landlady before Cook had bid her farewell. It had been a sombre morning because Ella didn't know if she would ever see the kindly older woman again. All night she'd lain awake, waiting for Clara to drag her back. Her absence at the house would have been noted by now and the knowledge that she'd created danger for Milly made her feel queasy.

Before she had time to contemplate her options, she was pressed onto the omnibus and sat amongst the passengers who watched warily.

London itself was a cacophony of sights and sounds, horses' hooves clattering on the cobbles, mixed with the chatter of costermongers and the hawking laughter of patrons spilling out of public houses.

The buildings that lined the streets were tall and narrow, the shopfronts changing from affluent dress-makers and grandiose hotels in the city, to ship chandlers and merchants' offices the closer she got to the waterside.

The open streets around the docklands were stocked with equipment for the ship or for the sailor. The grimy windows of the shops were filled with bright, brass chronometers and huge Mariner's compasses, and the flap of cheap canvas clothing covering the shop fronts of the shoe-mart. Slop-sellers lingered on the street corners; their carts sitting in muddy puddles though were piled high with meat and shellfish designed to fill the bellies of passing trade.

Despite the frenzied activity, there was a sense of danger that looked in the shadows. Ella ducked her head into her shoulders as she made her way closer to the maritime centre, aware of the menacing men loitering in the shadows, their eyes scanning the crowds for easy targets.

She moved with the urban flow of people, following the directions given to her by the omnibus conductor.

Ella stood to one side as a scrawny boy rolled an empty cask along the stones, the drum-like sound rumbling past her. She bumped into a wooden cage, jumping back when a goat bleated at her in protest. She was turned around as she bounced off several people before she lost her footing and fell backwards, landing heavily into a pile of sacks.

"I wouldn't sit down there for too long, lass," the Irish brogue behind her was gravelly with smoke and age. "The men around here aren't too fussy, and those sacks are bound for the Indies."

Ella bounded up and grabbed her small case, the apology dying on her lips as she turned to the voice. The man's face was the colour of worn leather, his right eye clouded white, the other warm brown as it twinkled up at her. He watched her as his gnarled fingers expertly wove the twine fibres of the net in his hands back together.

"Forgive me," Ella said. "I lost my footing."

The old man grinned at her, smooth pink gums revealing a few brown teeth still hanging on there for grim death. "It's no bother to me," he replied. "Speaking to a pretty girl makes a change from hollering at the scrawny street rats who want a coin for one of me nets."

The man's threadbare clothing was as filthy as his

face. He sat on a crate, his right leg missing from the knee down, a wooden stump stretched out in front of him in its place. He tapped his knee and grinned once more when he saw where she was staring. "Lost that to a shark," he boasted.

Ella didn't know where to put herself and rushed to apologise for staring at him. The old man shrugged and returned to his task. Ella hovered until he angled another look up at her. "What is it?"

"I'm looking for a public house," she said tentatively. "A pub called the Jolly Jack? Have you heard of it?"

His gaze turned from irritated to curious as his hands stilled. "What does a lass like you want to go in a place like the Jolly Jack for? Surely things aren't all that bad now."

"Please, sir. Some directions if you can. I was told to head down to London Docks and follow the smell of despair." The driver and his conductor had given her dire warning of venturing alone anywhere near the docks, but she had no choice. "Do you know of the place?"

"There ain't a point in this city where I don't know," he admitted. "But I can tell you right now, the likes of an innocent young thing like you will be gobbled up and spat out in a place like that in seconds."

A tremor shivered along her spine. "Nevertheless," she pressed on, "I need to find it, and I'd appreciate any help you can give." She reached into a pocket and removed a ha'penny, offering it to the man on an open palm.

The bright brown eye moved from her hand back up to her face. His wiry brow lifted. "What kind of business do you have there, lass?"

"A business that doesn't concern you," Ella replied sternly. For a moment, she thought that he would yell back at her, but he guffawed and waved away the coin.

"The Jolly Jack is away down the street. Go past the Talbot yard. The railway and shipping office will be on your right, you'll find the Jolly Jack on your left at the water's edge. If you're still alive, you can buy me a dram tonight. And lass?" He called out as she set off. Ella looked back at him. "Tell them old Finney sent you. It might buy you a little time before you're relieved of the rest of the coins in that bag in your pocket."

Ella didn't know how Finney knew that her pocket contained the leather pouch that Cook had her given yesterday. With a sense of foreboding, she thanked the old man and re-joined the flow of people.

Beneath the grime of the shopfronts, she found the offices that he talked about. The exterior of the Jolly Jack was faded, its red brickwork blackened with time. The front door was propped open, and the smell of stale ale and roasted meat wafted out onto the street, mingling with the sweet scent of tobacco smoke.

She approached the front of the pub, studiously ignoring the caterwauling and barks of approval made by the rough-looking people loitering outside. Inside, she could see groups of men huddled around the tables, playing cards, or throwing dice. Jaded women in washed-out dresses languished over the bar, flirting as they chatted with the regulars. The noise inside was deafening, the clinking of glasses and raucous laughter filling the air.

Dark wooden timbers crowded the low ceiling, and the roughly hewn timber flooring was covered with sawdust underfoot. The bare brick walls had been whitewashed. Low windows let in what was left of the daylight, their black frames broken into quadrants. Beyond the glass, she could see the river's dark waters filled with boats.

Heart pounding, Ella ventured further inside. She squawked when a thick arm dropped unceremoni-ously along her shoulder. She stared in horror at a set of beady eyes that peered out from underneath the hank of filthy black hair. Most of the man's face was obscured by a thick black beard. The pungent stink of fish oil filled her senses as the man leaned closer to her and murmured in her ear, "How much for the hour?"

Ella mewled and tried to move away, shaking her head as her mind scrambled to think of a suitable way of extricating herself from his grasp.

"There you are, my dear." She heard a smooth voice interject from behind. "If you'd be so kind as to step back from my fiancée, good sir."

"Fiancée, you say?" The sailor growled whilst grin-ning at Ella.

"That's right. And if you value your job, you'll do as I say right now or I shall have no choice, but to visit your captain and ensure that you're thrown off my ship."

The beady eyes darted up. "Mr Milford, sir, didn't see that it was you!" The odious sailor lifted his arms in surrender and merged with the pulsating group behind him, a rushed apology tumbling from his lips.

Ella turned and found herself looking into a pair of earnest eyes, the colour of obsidian. His dark hair was swept back of his face, and high cheekbones made his handsome face that much more interesting. He wore an exquisitely cut suit, a crisp white shirt offset by a claret cravat at his throat. His carriage told her that he was someone used to being obeyed. The harsh cut of his mouth softened as he smiled, and he inclined slightly in a bow as he introduced himself.

"Seth Milford," he said, holding out his hand.

Ella tried to get her heart rate back under control as she laid a trembling hand on his. "Thank you, sir," she said.

Seth held her hand as his eyes roamed her face, taking in the rosy flush of her cheeks and clear blue gaze. His eyes lingered a moment longer on full lips before they returned to her eyes once more. He leaned forward, and added conspiratorially, "This is usually the part where you tell me your name."

"My name is Ella," she replied, deliberately skirting the subject of her identity as Cook's dire warnings about Clara echoed inside. She knew just how furious her stepmother would be, especially as Ella had information that could disrupt her plans to access the Seward's vast wealth.

Seth released her hand, a dark brow winging up. "No surname? Or are you a woman of mystery?"

"If she's not a Tomlinson, I'll be a monkey's uncle." A deep voice boomed.

Ella spun in surprise. A wide-set, stout man stood behind the bar, but his blue eyes were as familiar to her as the back of her hands. His brown hair was long and tied with a leather thong at the nape of his neck. His shirt was loose muslin cloth rather than the expensive cotton that Henry used to wear, and his wide hands wore callouses from his line of work, but she would have recognised his smile anywhere.

"Hello, Uncle James."

CHAPTER 15

*H*er uncle's lowly sitting room was a stark contrast to the elegance and refinement of where Henry had entertained his guests. It was a small and cramped area, with threadbare carpets and worn furniture fighting for space. The room was cluttered with books and papers, and a scarred table cowered in the corner.

She wasn't sure what she would find when she'd set out to find her father's younger brother, nor had she given much consideration to her delivering the news that Henry had died. She'd certainly not expected such abject grief. Her uncle filled the high back chair, his gaze unseeing as he stared through the window to his right.

She could hear the boisterous activity of the tavern below, and the clang and thrum of the docklands beyond the windows but the atmosphere in the smoky room was thick with emotion. She could see such similarities between the brothers, although James' vernac- ular wasn't as polished. It made her heart ache even more for what she'd lost.

Maud, James' plump wife, poured tea from a chipped teapot. Ella had caught the other woman staring at her with open curiosity more than once.

"We don't get much cause to entertain family," she said by way of apologising for the state of the room. "And I've not met any of James' side before."

Ella was perched on the edge of a rickety chair; its red velvet arms having rubbed down to bare cloth.

"Well, there's only her left now," James mumbled, his tortured gaze reaching across the room. "All those years we didn't speak… I thought we had more time."

Ella felt her eyes burn with shared grief. She looked at her hands and had to relax her fingers. "So did I."

"You have the look of your mother, Ella. I knew it was you soon as I clapped my eyes on you. Caught me on the hop, thought I was seeing a ghost in my bar," James said softly.

His words pierced her bruised heart. There were times when hearing that she looked like Elizabeth Tomlinson helped, and other times that made her wish her mother had survived the terrible disease that had ended her life so abruptly.

James waited for her to respond but she couldn't, so he said, "I'm surprised that Clara allowed you to tell me about my brother. I suppose she's outside? I really can't see her lowering her standards enough to grace us with her presence, and never in a public house." Her uncle's tone was bitter as he reached for the cup of tea that Maud held out to him.

Ella debated how much she should tell her uncle. Although his reception so far had been welcoming, she still wasn't sure why the brothers had fallen out in the first place. Their letters hinted at their differences, but the initial contact appeared to have been from Henry telling James that he'd been right all along.

Ella was suddenly nervous. Up until that moment, her focus had only been on getting here. Now came the real test – would her uncle offer her shelter after all the bad blood that he'd shared with Henry? "I'm here alone, uncle," she said slowly, gauging his reaction.

Even Maud straightened up to stare at her. "Alone? In London? Why would she do that to you?"

"Where is Clara?" James demanded.

Ella's lips rolled inwards as her internal debate waged on. Unbidden, her eyes filled with tears.

James set the cup in his lap. He seemed to share his brother's astute stare. "There's much more to this story than you're letting on, Ella. The last I heard from Henry, he claimed to be having troubles, though he didn't explicitly say what they were about, only that he was having to move quickly." He added sugar to the cup, and stirred it slowly, thoughtfully, before he set the spoon down.

Ella nodded. "I know. I found your letters in his business-room. It's how I knew where to find you. Before then, I didn't know that you were even alive, let alone that Papa was in contact with you. Originally, I'd planned on writing to you but… I had to rethink my plans."

"Where is Thomas?" He asked.

"I need your help," she whispered, eyes downcast.

Untouched, James set the cup on the floor in front of him. He leaned forwards and fixed her with a stark look. "I think you'd better start talking, my girl. And fast."

So, she did. Her uncle didn't say a word whilst she spoke. She told him about the way her father had spoken his name with his dying breath, but that Clara had sent her from the room, even as Henry was trying to convey a message to her. James' jaw flexed in time with his huge fists, and still, he listened.

She told him about the upcoming nuptials of Clara to the wealthy Dr Seward who was also the man who'd treated her father for his many ailments but who was unable to explain the cause of death when Ella had asked; about how she'd been locked up and promised to a man she'd only met twice so that Clara could cleanse her house of Tomlinson's. And finally, about how she suspected that Thomas wasn't her kin at all and that Clara would be furious that someone who knew her deepest secret had escaped her clutches.

"I suspect she'll come looking for me. I don't know if she knows where you live–"

"Oh, she knows," James' laugh was brittle and bitter.

"Then I fear I've brought trouble to your door, too, uncle, and for that, I'm truly sorry. I will go if you like."

"No, you'll stay here with us."

Ella's relief was palpable yet short-lived when her aunt interrupted, "No, I don't think so, James. We can't afford to feed another mouth when we can barely feed ourselves."

James quietened his wife's protests with a single look. "I will not turn away Henry's girl, Maud. She stays."

Maud banged her cup onto the table and raised her voice, "I'm not fetchin' and carryin' for her sort! I have enough to do around here without playing nursemaid to some spoiled brat!"

"Aunt, please," Ella interrupted her. "I can work."

"Likely bleedin' story," Maud snorted, folding her arms huffily. "I heard all about your kind. Can't even dress properly without someone there to hold the dress for you to step into."

"You're right," Ella capitulated. "I have grown up in a house where we had maids – but they were incredibly hard-working folks who were proud of their careers and without whom a house as large as ours wouldn't have been able to function. They even helped my father raise me. Cook is the one who helped me escape and I dread to think about what's happened to my friend Milly – yes, another maid – w-who no doubt has been made the scapegoat for my absence," Ella caught herself as her words desperately tumbled over each other.

"My father came from humble beginnings and raised me to know that to get anywhere in life, you had to graft for it. He instilled that in *both* of his children," she whispered fiercely as emotion crowded in on her, her tears falling hot and fast.

She would never know if her father had been aware of Thomas's parentage but if he had, he never let it show in how he raised the boy. "I'll work, aunt. I have a strong back. I can clean, light fires… I can even do a little bit of cooking, though not on the scale that you'd need to feed the number of people downstairs, I'll admit. I will do my own fetching and carrying." She implored her aunt with a look, linking her fingers together and holding them in front of her in supplication. "Please, aunt. I have nowhere else to go. Please don't make me go back there."

Maud's lips flattened before she stood up and huffed from the room. James waited a beat after the door had been slammed into the frame before he spoke, "Don't mind her. Her bark is worse than her bite."

Ella wiped her eyes quickly, trying to gain some composure back. "I don't blame her. It must be disconcerting for her to have family arrive suddenly on her doorstep."

A smile hovered around the edges of James' mouth, his eyes twinkling as he looked back. "You know, Miss Ella, if you're going to fit in here, you can't go around using big words like *'disconcerting'*. You're in a London Docks public house now, my girl."

∾

IN THE EVENING, the Jolly Jack came alive.

The turbulent crowd filled the space to brimming, the boisterous shouts and clinking glasses combining into a deafening clamour.

Ella trembled in the corner, trying to make herself as small as possible, to remain unnoticed. She'd never seen a sight quite like it.

The public house was a popular spot for sailors, boatbuilders and watermen, trying to outdo each other as they swapped tales of daring adventures on the high seas. Their faces were weathered by the sun and salt air, their bodies strong and lean from years of hard work. The air was thick with the smell of tobacco smoke and the sweet tang of beer. Despite its disordered appearance, the Jolly Jack seemed a place of camaraderie; a haven for those seeking shelter.

James and Maud were behind the bar, their movements fluid and well-practised as they served their high-spirited patrons. The other barmaid, who'd introduced herself as Elsie slipped in between the two owners. Elsie poured pint after pint of ale and drams of whiskey without breaking her stride. Vivid eyes and a ready smile added an allure to the redheaded woman, though Ella had already seen her put one amorous sailor back in his place with a sharp tongue lashing.

The longer Ella watched them all work, the more she realised that she couldn't possibly stay here and earn her keep. Their movements were certain, and she could tell just how comfortable they all were here whereas Ella flinched with every bark of laughter or shout ringing out over the crowd.

From her vantage point, Ella spotted those who lurked in the shadows, their eyes scanning crowds. Without trying, she could picture the trouble brewing, even before the man playing cards to her left upended the table, sending cards and drinks scattering with an almighty crash.

Frozen in fear, James cursed colourfully at the men who began to fight. He lifted back the hatch of the thick oak bar and waded through the sea of burly men. He easily plucked up the drunken man who was raging at another and calling him a cheat, dragging him through the writhing crowd. She covered her mouth as the man was sent sailing through the front door.

James dusted off his hands and then executed a low bow to welcome in another customer who'd had to stand back to allow the drunkard to be ejected.

"What about yer, James? Did yer not like the colour of his coin, man?" Old Finney cackled as he hobbled in. A small smile curved her lips as she recognised the man who'd been sitting on the crate and weaving his nets earlier.

Ella missed the response from her uncle as the crowd volume started up again, but the heart-warming greetings and back-clapping acceptance between her uncle and Finney spoke volumes. The crowd seemed to eddy and part around the old man so that he could make his way across the room.

She stood on top tiptoes and tried to gain his attention so that when the man slipped his arm around her waist, she was caught off-balance. With a cry, she dropped unceremoniously into his lap and was immediately enveloped in a sour stench of whiskey. She turned her face away as he leered at her, "Hello, lass, where have you been all my life?"

Knowing that her uncle wouldn't be able to see her from this angle, she began to struggle in earnest as his meaty hands explored her slight frame. "If you can just let me up, please, sir… stop! Sir, please!"

He either ignored her or couldn't hear her above the din as he nuzzled her neck. His hand slipped higher up and grabbed her breast through her bodice. Instead of fear, Ella was filled with fury and her hands shot out to try and get purchase from any surface around here. Fingers instinctively closed around the first surface that she touched, and she brought the wooden tray down on the man's head.

His bellow of pain deafened her. As he flexed his body and put his hands to his head, Ella shot out of his lap. His comrades roared with laughter, pointing at his disgruntled expression, even as he cursed her and rubbed his crown, "Ye wee cow!"

"You keep your hands to yourself," Ella yelled primly at him.

Elsie arrived at her side, collecting up the tankards and tray, then draped a creamy arm along her shoulders. Ella braced for the scalding, but Elsie was grinning at her.

"That's my girl!" She howled and nodded at the

grousing sailor, "You'd best keep your hands to yourself, Mickey O'Shay! This is James' niece and he'll be none too pleased that you've made her crack one of his good trays over your thick bonse!"

Elsie gave her a quick squeeze and then she disappeared into the crowd, weaving, her way expertly through the maze of tables and grabbing hands.

Ella lifted the hatch of the bar and stepped behind the comparative safety. Maud leaned in, raising her voice to shout down at her ear, "Watch me and learn fast. And try and keep up!" She slid the glass under the tap and hauled on the lever as the light-brown liquid pooled in the bottom. Two more pulls and Maud slapped the glass down with one hand as the other slid another glass under the spout.

The piano in the corner was brought to life, and it was the quick strands of the fiddle that made Ella look up from her concentration. A ragtag band of musicians had struck up a lively tune, led by the animated Finney on the fiddle. His hands sawed out the jig and his good foot tapped along. Ella couldn't help the smile that slid over her face as the warm wood of the fiddle glowed in the low light.

She felt a little bit of her uncertainty slip away as she got caught up in the melody. Ella drew her first glass of ale from the barrel as the rowdy men were now joined by the familiar verse of the sea shanty. And somehow, she knew that Henry Tomlinson would've approved.

lla

THE THICK OAK door creaked as Ella opened it, stepping through into the murky morning. The damp air was sharply scented with salt water and fish, and she could hear the river gently lapping the quayside as she climbed up the steps from the cellar door.

As the low light of dawn hazed through the thick fog, Ella could make out the warehouses looming through the gloom like forlorn spectres. For just a moment, in the quiet stillness of the morning, it seemed as if the docklands had paused to catch its breath, though she knew that it wouldn't be long before the narrow streets would be bustling again. She pushed her wicker basket into the crook of her elbow and adjusted her shawl higher up her neck to fend off the morning chill before she set off for the markets. She'd tucked her dark hair up into a pleat and covered it with a bonnet, the same grey as her dress.

Along the dank, cobbled lanes, she hurried around the stinking piles of rubbish that lay strewn across her path. She'd committed the route to the market to memory, yet her heart still raced at being out alone and unchaperoned. She'd been charged with fetching the ingredients for Maud's kitchen. Haddock, eels and oysters, though she knew that the trawlers wouldn't be docking just yet and so she'd go to the markets first for flour and sugar. Maud said that the best quality was put out first, though Ella wasn't sure how true this was. Perhaps Maud just wanted to make sure that her niece didn't laze in bed too long. Wagons and carts trundled along the road, and she had to pause to allow two riders to pass her by, their iron-shod hooves sending sparks flying off the cobbles as they rode.

She wound her way through the narrow passageways, careful to keep her gaze down so as not to attract unwanted attention from the filthy faces loitering in doorways and on the street corners. Spitalfields marketplace was alive with activity, a hubbub of commercial commotion by the time she got there. Fruit and vegetables were stacked high on the stalls, the sellers hawking their wares so that their voices combined in a cacophony.

Ella followed the list that Maud had left, including the prices she should be paying. The negotiations were unnerving but the coins on her palms when she held

ANNIE SHIELDS

them out were grudgingly snapped up. She even paid a ha'penny to two scraggly children clutching sprigs of fresh rocket and called by the bakery for fresh bread.

By the time she was heading back toward the docks, the sun had burned off the fog, revealing the blackened buildings and spikes of masts. Coffee smells drifted out of the fashion coffee houses that had replaced some of the older dens. A yelp caught in her throat when something furry and alive darted across her path, though it was a sleek black cat, not a rat, that leapt up the wall, a silver fish clamped its jaws. The cat seemed to gloat at her before it slunk over the other side and disappeared.

A smile touched her mouth when she spotted old Finney sitting on his upturned crate, his lap hidden beneath the netting that he was working on.

"You're away early today, lass!" He called out in his gravelly voice.

She held the basket aloft. "On my way back."

"That uncle of yours is working you hard, I see!"

She drew alongside him and set the basket at her feet to give her arm a rest. "Do you ever sleep, Finney? It must have been the small hours before you'd finished playing last night."

She'd been cleaning up before James had sent her to bed, and she could still hear the din through the floor-boards until exhaustion had finally claimed her. She'd been living with her uncle for barely a week, and the change in routine was hard to adjust to. Her days were long and arduous, but she felt useful for the first time in her life. In the docks, people knew James Tomlinson well and the regulars were starting to recognise her.

He angled his head up and grinned at her. "I loves playing my fiddle, lass. Hardly call it work, now, would yer?"

James made special provisions of food for Finney whenever he was in the Jolly Jack. Sailors and traders made a point of stopping by the pub whenever Finney was playing his sprightly tunes.

"Besides," the old man shrugged, his attention returning to his work, "I'll get enough sleep when I'm dead."

Ella laughed. "Will we see you later?"

"What's in your basket?"

"Vegetables. She's making a mutton stew," Ella lifted her basket and settled it on her arm again. "Hare soup and rabbit pie."

Finney smacked his lips. "Aye, I'll be there, lass. Save me a piece of that pie!"

She waved goodbye and made her way down to the quayside. The foul stench of fish grew stronger, and she saw the baskets of lobsters waiting on the side, the blue-black prisoners awaiting their fate.

The fishmongers called out their wares in a boister-ous, melodic singsong, enticing customers to peruse their offerings. Ella found herself pausing for a moment, the beauty of the iridescent scales and the bright-eyed stares of the fish captivating her.

She jostled with the market sellers and traders for fresh oysters and haddock. They were wrapped in newspaper and added to her heavy basket. The quay-side was busier now, filled with sailors and warehouse workers, loading the boats and taking off cargo. Cranes did the heavy work, and drays awaited at the quays. But it was the colossal steamship in the harbour that drew her gaze.

Its black iron hull and rusty-red band around the bow, with four enormous masts and twin banded funnels set it apart from other passenger liners she'd seen disgorging its contents before now. This ship dwarfed everything else in the docks. She took a step forward, but something snagged her arm and yanked her back, just as a wagon rolled past her, its driver letting loose a string of expletives that would make even the hardiest sailor blush.

Ella turned to thank the person who'd saved her from going under the wheels of the cart and her gaze collided with a familiar one.

"Mr Milford!" she said. "It seems I am in your debt once again. Thank you."

His hand lingered on her elbow a touch longer than was needed as if he was assuring himself that she was steady on her feet before he removed his hat, smoothing a hand over his dark hair. "Are you alright?" he asked with a look along the street. "I'm afraid some folks around here don't care much for proprietary ways."

She laughed, unnerved by the tingling sensation where his fingers had been. "Yes, I'm fine. I'm still adjusting to the colourful use of language, but I'll live. I was distracted by that huge ship."

His dark bow hooked up. "You thinking of leaving us for America?"

"No, sir," she mumbled. "It's just… well, it's enormous."

"The SS Britannic. No doubt in London for some work on the engine that was built in Lambeth. She usually docks in Liverpool. She holds the Blue Riband for the fastest average speed both East and West across the Atlantic. She is a sight, isn't she?"

Ella blinked at him, watching the admiration shimmering in his expressive eyes as his dark gaze ran over the gargantuan ship. "She? Do boats have a gender?"

"Well, like a woman, a ship is unpredictable," Seth laughed and settled his hat back on his head. "At least, that's the old saying amongst sailors. Traditionally, boats are given female names because they nurture men deep inside and protect them on their crossing. I could probably bore you with the Latin meaning of such things and their feminine origins but it's hardly the right environment for a school lesson."

From his twinkling eyes and wide smile, Ella could tell that Seth Milford was aware of the effect he had on women. He'd lowered his voice and closed the gap between them a little so that her heart fluttered in her chest in response to his proximity.

He straightened up and pointed behind him. "Sorry, my family is in shipping – those are my offices behind you."

Ella looked in the direction he indicated. Milford Shipping building was much the same as every other office clustered around the wharf. Through the wide arched windows on the ground floor, she could see books and papers piled on the ledge, and she imagined ledgers and cabinets filled with much the same.

"You're a bit of a mystery to the locals, you know."

His comment brought her head back around quickly. She searched his face, wondering more about his family. If his family had connections to Oxford or Bath, neither was all that far away in the scheme of things. "I am?"

"Of course," he replied genially, unaware of the unease rippling through her. "No one knew that James Tomlinson had a family."

Ella smiled her relief. She was so used to others having an agenda that she'd forgotten about the simple human need to just know. She could deal with genuine curiosity. "My father passed away recently. I am grateful to my uncle for offering me a place to shelter when I needed it."

"I'm so sorry to hear of your loss," Seth said candidly. His sincerity made her throat tighten and she could only nod.

"You've lost your father, too?"

His mouth flattened and he shook his head. "My father is the head of the business. We spend most days locking horns over even the most trivial of issues, I'm afraid. I feel that I am a constant source of disappointment to him. My mother is the peacemaker between us, though she too can be a source of aggravation when the mood takes her.

I have friends who are orphaned and who've had to throw themselves on the pity of estranged family, so I can sympathise with your loss. I'd be happy to show you around the local area one day. Perhaps give you a tour away from the unprincipled miscreants who'd yell at a lady on a fine spring morning?"

She fidgeted as her mind tried to think of a way to let him down gently. "That's a very kind offer, Mr Milford, but–"

"Don't answer now," he added quickly. "It's just I… well," his chin dropped, and his smile was captivating and self-effacing. "I would like to get to know you more."

Ella stared at him, speechless. A man who looked the way he did, interested in her? Or had he more nefarious reasons for wanting to get to know her?

"Ella!" Maud's voice cut through the hubbub of the street. Ella jolted and saw her aunt at the corner of the street, her hand shielding her eyes from the sunlight. "Will you get a move on? How can I make a pie without the ruddy flour, girl?"

Ella sent Seth an apologetic look. She hefted the basket to illustrate her point, "I must get back, Mr Milford."

"*Now*, Ella!"

"I'll be there at lunchtime!"

Seth lifted his hat once more and called out to her as she hurried away but she didn't answer him. As much as she'd like to explore the exciting sensations that he elicited in her, she couldn't risk Clara discovering her.

"Sorry," Ella said to Maud as she reached her.

Maud continued to scowl behind Ella, and she risked a glance back. Seth hadn't moved. He sent them a cheery little wave before he turned and headed for his offices.

"Don't be getting taken in by his kind," Maud muttered, giving Ella a shove in her back. "They only ever want one thing."

Ella walked around the corner, steadying the basket with her free hand. "What do you mean?"

Maud rolled her eyes. "You can't be that naïve, girl. Seth Milford is rich, spoiled and used to getting what he wants. I've seen his type a hundred times."

Ella found herself wanting to defend him, even though she'd reached the same summary of his character. "He was telling me about the ships. He saved me from nearly going under a wagon."

"Then you need to pay more attention, and not to handsome, wealthy men who are only looking for fun," Maud hurried her along the cobbles. "You'll be just a notch on a bedpost for them, whereas a woman is left with the consequences of their philandering ways.

Very often, they already have a wife who enjoys the privilege and protection of a man. Men who look like him also have a mistress who keeps their bed warm in every port. You're here to work hard and hide from your stepmother," she added with a low undertone. "Now, did you fetch all the ingredients I asked for?"

"Yes, I did."

"Thank heavens for small mercies," Maud muttered and put her shoulder into the back door of the cellar to open it.

Ella passed by her, grateful to be able to hide the reaction her aunt's words had brought up. That he only wanted to get to know her for one reason. She wouldn't be a notch on anyone's bedpost.

CHAPTER 17

*S*eth

SETH WATCHED Ella hurry away as if chased by the devil himself. He imagined that none of the things her aunt was saying to her was flattering – at least not about him, judging by the dark look. He couldn't help sending the old battle-axe a cheery little wave. Her only saving grace was that she cooked like an angel.

He made his way across the street, weaving between carts and barrels, his mind lingering on the pretty newcomer. She wasn't the usual type of woman to be found in the docklands. She possessed an inno-cent air though she was nervous as a cat that hears a mouse in the wall. Though he couldn't say exactly what it was about her that he found alluring. She was pretty enough, but he was surrounded by pretty women. A heart-shaped face and blue eyes that he would lay good money on hiding something in their depths.

"Morning, Mr Milford!" Charles Graves called out as Seth let himself in through the office door. The clerk was sitting at his desk, surrounded by piles of documents. The man was small and mousy but had an insightful mind.

"You're in early, Charles," Seth hung up his coat and hat.

Milford Shipping Office reflected its wealth and prestige. Maps of the world covered the walls, showing the routes that their ships took to all corners of the globe. His father's office was upstairs, away from the noise and bustle of the dockyard. Shipping manifests were spread out over Seth's desk and his leather chair creaked as he lowered himself into it.

"The Lady Michelle docked this morning," Charles replied. "I'd heard that they had made good time, so I thought I'd come down in case it was more than a rumour."

Seth paused to look up. "That's a very good time. Thank you, Charles."

"Favourable tides, it seems. Anyway, the captain was keen to be paid after a successful voyage."

"Of course," Seth said. "We need good captains. Did he say if there were any issues with the crossing?"

"He said it was the smoothest he'd had."

"Saint Nicholas has favoured us," Seth replied with a chuckle. "Is the stock ready to go again?"

Charles's mouth compressed. "Not yet, no. I'm led to believe the barge will be with us later today."

"That's good. Let me clear my desk and then I shall be with you."

The morning passed quickly. Milford Shipping employed several clerks and secretaries who dealt with the paperwork. Seth reviewed reports and signed documents, overseeing payments, and calculating the costs of shipping. Captains came and went, with stories of their adventures at sea, avoiding pirates and battling storms. Despite the chaos, Seth remains focused.

This was where he thrived. His mind focused on what needed to be done for the good of the company. No idle gossip. He knew every detail of the business and was considered a master with an eye for details.

As lunchtime rolled around, Seth stood and stretched his back muscles, his stomach growling. Grey clouds had rolled in, and he could smell the rain in the air. He retraced his steps towards the Jolly Jack, looking forward to Maud's delicious food whilst watching the pretty new barmaid.

He'd already had a successful morning. His ship arrived almost two days earlier than planned, and a good deal was secured on a trade with a new company at the East India dock. And now he'd spend his lunch watching the very pretty Ella Tomlinson. He found her charming, more so when she blushed as he leaned in.

If he could just get her to agree to take a stroll with him, then he'd consider it a great day all around.

CHAPTER 18

lla

ELLA PREFERRED the days at the Jolly Jack.

They were just as busy as the evening trade, with merchants and traders seeking out tasty fare and good ale to fill their bellies. But it was easier. There were certainly fewer foraging hands from drunken sailors to avoid and the punters were generally happier too. No brawls or scraps to clean up after.

Knives and forks scraping the plates and clinking of tankards could be heard above the raucous chatter, as sailors who'd arrived earlier were already spending their coin as they waited for the next sail. Stevedores gathered around tables before they headed back to the doss house for the day.

Elsie was hurriedly pouring pints for the thirsty

dock workers. She moved with practised ease, juggling the frothy tankards and coins expertly. It was Ella's job to run the food to the table and to clear the dirty plates away so that the next customers could fill the places. The two of them had found their rhythm of working together as the weeks passed by.

"You're going to meet yourself coming back at this rate," Old Finney chuckled as Ella trotted past him.

She brushed back a lock of hair that curved around her jaw and shot him a quick smile. "You know how she gets if there's a dirty table."

"Aye, I know."

Maud was in the kitchen, dishing out the last of her mutton stew. Ella dumped the plates in the sink, grateful that they'd hired a pot washer for the day. The young girl was standing on a bucket, skinny legs poking out of boots that were too big for her. But she worked hard and without complaint, happy to have been given some work for the day.

"You're doing a grand job," Ella told the young thing and was rewarded with a shy smile.

"She is," Maud agreed. "Might be more work again tomorrow if you don't break anything."

Ella sent the girl a wink and whirled out of the kitchen once more. She spotted Seth the second he ducked through the front door, her pulse kicking up a notch in response to him. His white collar contrasted with his jet-black hair, and she knew the second his eyes settled on her by the involuntary shiver that raced across her skin.

"Afternoon, Mr Milford," she said to him. He was a regular to the Jolly Jack. However, he was the only one who seemed to have this effect on her.

His smile upped and she cursed her racing heart. "Hello, again, Miss Tomlinson."

"Take a seat, I'll be right with you," she said, noting that he took the table next to the window.

"No rush," he replied and made himself comfortable.

She headed to Finny and scooped up his bowl. "How was it?"

"As good as I remember," Finny replied.

"I'll let Maud know. Are you playing tonight?"

"I'd play every night if I could. Nothing beats sharing the gift of music."

Ella smiled, even as a sliver of pain cut through her. She remembered the joy of playing her violin, of seeing the pleasure written on her father's face as he watched her. The flames destroyed her violin as Clara had burned it.

Finney's hand shot out, the movement belying his advanced age. "What is it, girl?"

His voice was laced with concern, and she was horrified to find her eyes stinging. She rolled her lips and swallowed twice to get herself back under control. "Nothing," she managed to whisper.

"Something," Finney murmured. "Enough to put shadows in your eyes."

Ella sighed and gave him a watery smile. "Not your fault."

ANNIE SHIELDS

"Ella?"

"I'm fine, Finney. I'll see you later?"

"Aye, okay, lass," he acquiesced though her retreat didn't give him much choice.

She quickly stowed his empty dishes before she made her way to where Seth Milford was sitting.

He watched her approach, a small line between his dark brows. "Did that man upset you?" He pointedly looked over the bar to where Finney was chatting with Elsie.

"Who, Finney?"

"Yes."

"No, not at all."

"I saw him manhandle you," he said roughly. "Did he say something to upset you?"

Ella shook her head. "He's harmless. A sweetheart, too."

A dark brow winged up. "Harmless? For someone who's been around the docklands as long as he has, I'd hardly call him harmless. A scoundrel, and a liar, perhaps, especially to grab at your wrist that way."

Ella stared at him, annoyance flickering at the edges of her temper. "He meant nothing by it, sir. Why would you call him a liar?"

"Because he tells anyone who'll listen that he lost the leg to a shark. He's a weaver. He has no place being on a boat," Seth scoffed. "When would it have been bitten off? I've never met a sailor who'd survive such an attack. If he lied about that, he's a man not to be trusted. What did he say to you to upset you and make you rush off?"

Ella glanced back to check that Finney couldn't overhear them. Finney had been nothing but lovely to her ever since she'd arrived. She looked out for him daily and enjoyed their chats. He was a fascinating man with a wealth of stories to tell. More importantly, he was her friend. Who cared if some were exaggerated for entertainment purposes?

When she met Seth's eyes again, she was ticked off. "I find it sad, Mr Milford, that you would cast such aspersions on a man's character. Have you ever had a conversation with him, and listened to what he had to say? I'm sure you'd be delighted by his tales."

Seth sat back in his chair, his face registering his surprise. "I meant nothing by it—"

"I speak as I find," she continued as if he'd not spoken. "I don't know what it was that I said or did that invited you to rush to my protection but, on this occasion, it's unfounded. Finney is a dear friend of mine. I could care less if he lost his leg to a shark or in a game of cards. He is a sweet, genuine man.

Now, if you've quite finished with the character assassination, we have mutton stew and hare soup left. The rabbit pie has sold out but there are fresh eels, too."

She didn't care if he was discombobulated from the telling-off. She kept her eyes on the table surface in front of him, ignoring the look he was sending her.

"Ella, if I offended you, I apologise."

"No need," she stated matter-of-factly. "What would you like to order?"

"Stew, please," Seth said. "And a glass of cider, if I can."

"Coming right up." She spun on a heel and stomped into the kitchen to place the order.

"What's got you so riled?" Elsie asked as she poured the cider for Seth.

Ella glared across the room. Seth was gazing through the window, to where the boats moved about on the river beyond. He stood out amongst the crowd in his sharp suit and clean-shaven face. He might send her pulse racing, but he'd annoyed her royally.

"Nothing I can't handle."

Elsie slapped the pint down and reached for the wooden tray, wiggling it playfully. "Need this to beat him with, too?"

Ella's mouth split for a grin, and she chuckled. "Not yet but keep it handy, just in case."

Elsie nodded, sending a quick grin at the sailor who'd arrived at the bar. As Elsie took the order, Ella carried the pint across the floor and set it down in front of Seth.

"Wait," he said, as she turned to leave. "I'm sorry. I had no idea you were so fond of Finney. I apologise if I've offended you, that was not my intention."

Ella placed a hand on her hip and pursed her lips at him, saying nothing.

Long fingers traced the edge of the tankard as those perceptive dark eyes of his moved to the bar and back.

"I saw him grab at you and you looked upset when you left. I don't like the thought of you being upset... by anyone," he added quietly.

Ella's irritation deflated. "Oh... well..." She could feel the pink infusing her cheeks under his careful stare. "He hadn't said anything offensive. Just something that made me remember something sad."

"I see," he said quietly. He studied the tankard and Ella began to fidget as the silence between them stretched on.

"Then perhaps I owe you an apology, too," she offered.

A hint of a smile softened his mouth, and she felt a tug low in her gut. She preferred the anger he'd invoked, it felt less dangerous than this insidious pull that he ignited in her.

"Apology accepted. I meant what I said, Ella. What I've said most days that I've been in here. I would like it if I could see you again... away from here, alone."

Alone with him? She took a step back before it had registered in her mind.

"I'm afraid that wouldn't be possible. We're terribly busy... every day."

Seth tried again, looking up at her through raised brows. "I can speak with your uncle. Assure him that my intentions are honourable. I find you very intriguing, Miss Tomlinson."

The noise level increased and some of the men who'd been in drinking since they'd opened were getting rowdy. Ella could have kissed their drunken heads and welcomed the intrusion. Dealing with them was certainly preferable to the penetrating stare that she was receiving.

"I'm flattered, Mr Milford. Truly, I am but… no. I must get back to work now."

The wild group distracted her and took some time to settle. However, when she looked across at his table again, Seth was watching her. He was chewing thoughtfully on a slice of bread that he'd dipped into the stew.

She quickly looked away and hurried to answer the bell that Maud used to let them know another order was ready. She should be flattered that a man of his standing would show such an interest but, after her experience with men like him, she wasn't interested in love, nor the potent feelings being near him brought out.

She liked work. Uninterrupted and uncomplicated work. And that's what she'd stick to.

CHAPTER 19

"Come on, you lot, don't yer have homes to go to?" James called out to the room in general.

The clock had struck midnight and a call for last orders had been made at the Jolly Jack, but it was still a herculean effort to empty the place of merry punters. The oil lamps flickered, casting shadows around the place, and lending a mysterious glow to it. Ella collected the empty cups and glasses, wiping down the bar as James helped the last few drunken sailors to their feet where they were slumped across the tables, fast asleep.

James set down some cups on the bar and said to Ella as she passed by him, "I think we can count tonight as a success."

Ella shot him a quick smile as she swiped a rag across the tabletop. The word 'we' brought a little warmth to her. She was starting to feel like she belonged here in this place, almost like she was part of a family once more. People respected her uncle and, other than the sailors who could flirt for England with her, she enjoyed herself here.

It was nights like tonight that she loved the most. Finney had spent the evening carousing on the corner stage with his friends, his elbow bobbing to the music as the customers had weaved and frolicked a jig. There had been dancing and merriment, and the place had been packed to the rafters not even an hour ago. Now, it was nearly empty as the last of the punters finished their drinks. Finney was sitting in his favourite chair by the fire – to warm his bones, he'd said – enjoying his free glass of whisky before bed, a small smile on his face as he stared into the hot coals.

"I would say so, uncle."

"You know," James said, coming to a halt in front of her. "I've been meaning to thank you. You've been a godsend to us, all told."

"In what way?"

"Well, helping with errands and the like. Running the food out and taking orders. Elsie has high praise for you, too, and she's a tougher nut to crack than Maud is."

Ella smiled, thinking that James might be slightly biased toward his wife, as Elsie was a pussycat compared to Maud's tongue-lashings. But neither had Clara's knack for being mean and cruel and for that she was thankful. She nodded and sidestepped, but James matched her, his face soft with compassion.

"I know we don't pay you much, but I just wanted

to point out that your hard work hasn't gone unnoticed."

Ella was relieved to hear such praise. "I'm grateful to you and Aunt Maud. I dropped in here unannounced, and you've been nothing but kind."

"Your father… he did a good job raising you, Ella."

She bit the inside of her cheek to keep the tears that stung her eyes from falling. "Thank you, uncle. I know that that would please him to hear it if he were here."

She thought he was about to say something else, but he seemed to change his mind. He cleared his throat and looked about the pub. "I can finish up here if you like."

Ella smiled and dunked the tankards he'd set down on the bar into a bowl of water. "I don't mind. Many hands make light work, you know."

The elevated brow made him look so much more like his older brother that it hurt her heart. "You're a good girl, Ella. A hard worker. But you should go to bed."

She looked about the room. She could see that the floor needed a sweep and the fire needed to die down more. "I'll finish up the glasses if you see to the stragglers. Plus looks like Finney is in for the night," she added with a grin.

The old man had dozed off, either from the warm hearth or the whisky. The glass was empty on the table next to him, his fiddle case at his feet. His arms were folded, and his head leaned against the back of the chair.

James rolled his eyes and huffed out a laugh. "Honest to God, he could sleep on a sixpence. Finney! Come on, man!"

Ella laughed as he didn't even rouse. James waved him off with dismissal and set about chivvying the rest of the people out of their seats. It had been a long and busy night, as it always was when Finney played. No doubt Maud had left her a list of tasks for the morning. Not that she minded. She enjoyed the newfound freedom and being the niece of James Tomlinson brought her a little bit of protection from those around the dockyard who were loyal to the landlord.

Soon enough, it was just Finney in his chair. With a hearty sigh, James went across to him and nudged him with his boot. "C'mon, Old Finney. Time to go home now."

Ella stored the tankards, looking up when James' voice grew sharper. With a sigh, she rounded the end of the bar, intent on using a kinder tone but drew to a stop when she saw the look of sadness on her uncle's face. Her gaze fell to Finney's slack expression, where he sat alongside the embers of the fire.

Tonight, Finney had played his last tune.

CHAPTER 20

The rain beat down relentlessly on the grey and grimy cobblestones. The procession of mourners filled the streets, passing by the empty crate where Finney had sat for years. Some doffed their caps; others left a flower. It had been that way ever since Finney's passing, as news of the tragedy spread through the community, though today it seemed that the thieves left the tokens sitting there alone out of respect.

She had only known old Finney for a short while, and yet his death affected her deeply. She would miss his kindness and his cackling laugh. Her tears had mingled with the rain when his body had been interred yet she didn't feel alone in her grief. Many gathered at the graveside, uncaring of the rain that pelted them as if the city itself mourned the loss of one of its own. The walk back from Old Saint's cemetery was a sea of black that weaved through the streets toward the docklands.

She realised that no one had turned away as the Jolly Jack came into view.

"I wonder what Finney would say if he knew that all of these people came to say goodbye to him," Ella murmured, her voice mingling with the hushed tones of the mourners.

James' mouth quirked in the corner. "He'd call us all fools for wasting money and that we should have dropped his body over the quayside, instead."

"But he set aside money for his funeral, obviously," Ella said. The horse-drawn hearse alone would cost a packet. "It was hardly a pauper's burial."

Her uncle shook his head. "Old Finney had no time for traditions."

"Then who paid for all this?" Maud demanded.

James' blue gaze moved over the crowd and settled on one spot. Ella followed the direction until she spotted a familiar face under his umbrella. "It was a collective effort, Maud."

Ella held Seth Milford's stare for a moment longer. She'd not seen him since he'd offered his condolences the morning after old Finney had passed away. She'd been standing in the doorway, shaken by watching his small, shrouded body being carted down the street. Seth had called her attention away from it. Even as he'd spoken words that she couldn't recall now, she'd known that the docks had lost a little of their sparkle.

"Come on," Maud groused. "Let's get this over with."

James ducked under the awning of the pub and

pressed the door back so that Ella could step through. "We'll raise a glass to him, shall we?"

Ella hung up her damp shawl and stoked up the fire to take the chill off the room as Elsie and Maud lit the candles and lamps about the room. The room behind them continued to fill. Sailors and watermen, boatmen and sack makers, superintendents, and merchants. All standing side by side. Old Finney had been a fixture in the docklands for as long as anyone could remember. His weathered face and lilting voice had been a constant presence, and now that he was gone, the place somehow seemed emptier.

As she reached the bar, she caught the eye of James, who nodded sympathetically. She could tell that he, too, was struggling with the loss of his friend. Without a word, he poured her a drink and pushed it across the bar.

"Right!" James' voice carried over the throng gathered in the Jolly Jack, strong despite his sadness. The group fell silent, turning expectantly to the landlord. "I think we can all agree that we thought that old bugger was immortal." A smattering of amused grunts moved through the people. "He survived many a storm at sea, having his leg bitten off by a shark–"

"I heard it was in old Davey Jones' locker, in exchange for at least one good eye!" One called out.

"He lost it to a giant octopus in the Indies!" said another.

"He told me it was pirates!"

Ella smiled, her gaze seeking out Seth in the sea of

faces. She found that he was looking right at her. He lifted a brow as if illustrating his point about the tales Finney had spun. She shrugged her response. She held his eyes a beat longer, wondering if he was the source of income for the funeral. And if he was, why did he do such a generous thing for an old man he thought to be beneath contempt?

The wavering light cast shadows on the faces of the men huddled in groups, nursing their drinks quietly, and Ella could hear them swapping stories and sharing memories of the old sailor. Before long, the Jolly Jack was a-buzz with voices.

James patted the air and laughed. "Well, I think we can all agree the old sea dog had a tale or two to tell. It was part of his charm, for although he had many a sea battle with the Kraken, he still had a heart of gold. I know the dockyard will never be the same.

We will miss him at the Jolly Jack. I know I shall miss the extra income from the nights he played," James shook his head playfully and laughter rippled through the crowds. "So, let's raise a glass to Old Finney."

Ella raised the glass to her lips, the bitter taste of the ale doing nothing to dispel the heavy cloud of sadness that filled her heart. She knew that life in the dock-lands would go on, much as life had after her father had died. Ships would continue to come and go, but it was going to be hard to imagine the Jolly Jack without him.

The voices chorused together as they all toasted

him, and she knew that Old Finney would love being the centre of attention. She said as much to James as he slapped his empty glass on the bar top.

"That's the truth," James said grudgingly. "He even left his fiddle here. It's behind the bar, I... I can't bring myself to part with it."

"Oh, please don't!" Ella couldn't help the alarm that pulled through her voice.

"You remember that your grandfather played?"

Her face creased with remembered anguish. "Papa had given it to me. Clara burned it. I was playing and she... she..." Ella shook her head, her throat closing off with emotion.

James growled and he leaned on the bar. "That woman is a witch."

"It's just... I know how much it would have meant to Finney. It should be on display here, as a tribute to him."

James reached below the bar and pulled out the battered case, setting it on the bar. His fingers tapped the case, then he flipped the small brass latches. The fiddle sat inside, just where Finney had set it a week ago. The wood seemed to gleam. "I can't put it on the wall. Some scallywag will have it away." He pushed the case toward her. "It should go to someone who will use it."

Ella shook her head. "I hardly knew him. I can't take it."

"Nonsense," James said. "He was fond of you. That

159

much I do know. He'd want it to go to someone who would use it. It's a shame to see it go to waste."

"Do you play, Ella?" Elsie asked as she came to a stop next to James. She'd been serving some of the punters but peered into the case.

"Of course, she does!" James crowed. "She has music in her blood. My father played, too."

"I play the violin," Ella said.

James rolled his eyes. "They're the same thing."

"Play something now for us?"

Ella shook her head. "I don't know any of the sea shanties."

"Then play something you do know," the quiet voice behind her pulled her around. Seth was close enough to touch. Close enough that her heart began to jump in her chest.

"I – I can't."

James leaned across the bar, a heavy brow arching up. "It'll be a fitting way to say goodbye to your friend."

"That's not playing fair, uncle," she admonished.

"This is London, my girl. There ain't nothin' fair in this city!" James cackled as he snatched up the fiddle case. "Finney has bequeathed the Jolly Jack with his fiddle. And would yer know it, we have a fiddler here in the bar!" A rousing cheer erupted across the crowd when he pointed at Ella's head. "Who here wants Ella to play a song? A fitting send-off for Old Finney, wouldn't you all say?"

No, not playing fair at all.

She looked at Seth for support, but he simply

shrugged and lifted his hands. She wanted to point out that she'd not played in months. That she knew nothing of the kind of music that the punters liked. Her heart pounding, she looked across the sea of faces. She was jiggled and jostled; words of encouragement were lost in the jackhammering pulse in her ears.

James set the case on the bar, his gloating grin and reassuring nod doing nothing to ease the panic pressing in on her.

"Can you play or not?" One clear voice asked her. The sound was soothing and calm. Ella nodded in response. His breath tickled her cheek. He was so close she could smell the soap he'd used. She met his gaze then. Seth's eyes were soft with compassion. She sucked in a breath to steady her nerves. "Then play what you know. Do it for your friend."

She wiped her palms down her skirts and then tentatively touched the fiddle. It was smooth and warm. Her fingertips skimmed the surface, and she couldn't help the smile that touched her lips.

Tenderly, she lifted the instrument out of the leather bed it lay in. It was smaller than her violin without any of the finesse that hers had had. And yet, she knew this little instrument could tell a story if it could, just like the man who'd owned it. The wooden body was scarred and chipped in places and yet, as she held it aloft and settled it between her chin and shoulder, the people closest to her pressed back to give her a little bit of space.

She aligned the bow to the strings, her heart in her

mouth and she closed her eyes. There she saw Finney's lopsided smile, grinning up at her, his milky eye now the colour of its mate, tawny and twinkling. And next to him, Henry, smiling, his eyes brimming with pride, the same way he always had when she'd played.

Instinctively, her fingers lay along the fingerboard, finding their positions. The room was silent, and she felt the expectation of the crowd. She drew the bow along the strings and the tune was sweet, as sweet, and as beautiful as she remembered it. *Jerusalem.* As good a send-off as she could think of. The music filled the room, and the strains of the voices pulled her eyes open. They sang for Finney, for themselves.

From Jerusalem, she played *A Kerry Dance.* Happy laughter filled the room and her heartache eased as her musical joy roared back to her.

Thank you, Finney, she thought. *I hope I do you proud.*

CHAPTER 21

"My head," Maud grumbled from beneath the damp cloth. She was lying on the sofa, hands folded across her stomach. It had been a long day for them all. First the funeral and then the impromptu party afterwards.

"Too much wine, old girl," James chuckled. "But I think we did old Finney proud."

He was in the chair closest to the hearth, his ankles crossed, watching the flames in the hearth. He looked across at Ella and asked, "Did you enjoy yourself?"

The church clock had struck two in the morning, and yet she still wasn't tired. Beyond the window, the world was dark. She could see the bright moonlight through the open curtains and knew that the scene beyond the window would appear ethereal in the light. They'd emptied the place at midnight after the music had continued all through the day and into the evening.

Ella hadn't played all night; there were some men only too happy to pick up the fiddle, yet it had been returned to her dutifully each time.

She set down her embroidery on the table in front of her as a smile ghosted her lips. "Would it be wrong with me to say yes, considering it was a funeral?"

James' eyes returned to the fireplace, his face a mix of shadows and glowing merriment. "Finney wasn't a man of tradition. He lived as full of life as any man I've ever met. I think he would appreciate the fact that it was more a celebration of him, rather than a maudlin affair."

The fiddle case was at the other end of the table. More than once last night, Ella had lost herself in the music. To find her forgotten joy once more brought on such a wave of nostalgia, but she found it hard to breathe.

"It still doesn't feel right to accept something of Finney's that must've held so much meaning to him, especially when I hardly knew him."

"Finney was hardly sentimental, my dear," James told her. "And in a small way, judging by the looks on everyone's faces tonight, it was as if he was still in the room with us. The only question I have for you though is how much do you intend to charge me for playing every night?"

"Goodness, no!" Ella's retort was immediate. "This was a mark of respect for Finney. That is all."

"But you have such talent," James replied, his face

bent with surprise. "A gift like that should be shared, especially when it can make you money."

Ella was still shaking her head. She couldn't picture herself repeating the performance. James sat forward, with his elbows on his knees as he directed a questioning book at her. "I'm offering you a job, Ella."

"I already have a job helping you out, uncle."

"I will pay you just as I paid Finney. Four shillings a night?"

Maud plucked the damp cloth off her face to angle a furious look at her husband. "You didn't pay Finney that much, did you?"

"Of course, not, dear," James retorted, pivoting in his seat to cut Maud out of the conversation, but Maud was like a bloodhound when it came to money.

"James?" Her voice was tight with anger. "You told me you paid him in stew and ale. That you had a gentleman's agreement. I never charged him a penny for what he ate and drank here! How much did you pay that wizened old man?"

"Mind your own business," James said impatiently.

"Don't you tell me to mind my own business! I graft here day in, day out–"

"The girl has talent, Maud," James snapped. "People will flock here to see her. I'm just being practical. The Jolly Jack is known for its entertainment. We need that for people to part with their coin, woman."

Ella had lived with her aunt and uncle long enough to know that the argument was escalating. James oversaw the business certainly, but Maud was no pushover. She had to put an end to this as she didn't want a quarrel to ruin Finney's night. "Arguing over how much Finney was paid is a moot point," she told them in as jovial a voice as she could muster. "Because I'm not doing it."

Maud glared at her before she settled back against her pillows and lay the damp cloth over her face once more. "Well, that is a shame because you have a talent worth sharing. Why wouldn't you want to help our business after everything we've done for you?"

Ella blinked, dividing a disconcerted look between them both. Her uncle leaned back on the arm of his chair, a cocky lopsided grin on his face. She wasn't sure how they could argue so much with each other and yet still stand united. Ella narrowed her eyes as she realised that she'd been manipulated.

The thought of standing up in front of people was both terrifying and exciting. She was meant to be keeping a low profile here, and yet Clara hadn't come battering down the door.

Perhaps Ella had done her favour, leaving the way that she did. Perhaps now Clara could live her life in the Tomlinson household with Dr Seward's money. She couldn't afford to think about what had happened before. She could only move forward, and she began to hope that her worry had all been for nothing.

Her eyes moved to the fiddle case. Even now, she could remember how wonderful it had felt to lose herself in the music, to disappear from everything around her and focus only on making her fiddle sing.

Finney has been such a fixture at the Jolly Jack that people remembered the pub whenever they came back to port. It was certainly an advantage to the other public houses in and around the dockyard.

"What do you say, Ella? Want to be the new fiddler at the Jolly Jack?"

Ella nibbled nervously at her lower lip. "What if I can't do it?"

"You did it tonight."

"Yes, but that was because people were here to say their goodbyes to Finney. What if I ruin your business?" She shook her head as fear overrode her. "Oh, no, Uncle. No, I couldn't take that risk."

"Very well," James acquiesced. "We'll try one night. See how it goes."

"For one shilling," Maud muttered behind her cloth.

James grinned and held up four fingers with a wink.

"WILL you be playing again tonight, Ella?"

Ella was concentrating on the motion of the beer engine, ensuring that the long poles on the handle were slow and rhythmic, just as Elsie had taught her. She gave John Tanner a quick smile before her hand pulled on the tap once more. "You'll have to call by and see, won't you, John?"

§John Tanner was a regular at the Jolly Jack, a boat builder with powerful shoulders and a friendly smile.

He was among just a few of the stragglers left in the bar now that the lunchtime rush had passed.

The bell tinkled from the kitchen, and all her Ella set the tankard down the bar top and took the payment for John's ale. When she walked into the kitchen, Maud pointed at the bowl of stew and two hunks of crusty bread on a plate next to it.

"That's the last of the stew," she said.

"It's quietening down now, anyway."

"I think I'll go for a lie-down if that's okay?"

Ella collected the stew and bread and gave her aunt an understanding look. "Will Uncle James be long? "

"Who knows, "Maud replied as she scrubbed at her face tiredly. "He calls it business but you and I both know he can talk the hind leg off a pot."

Ella backed out of the kitchen and carried the stew across the bar. Seth Milford had chosen a table that sat inside the curve of the bay window. It afforded him a view of the river. The May sunshine had made an appearance today, and the river sparkled invitingly between the boats and barges that moved through it.

He'd been every day in the past month for his lunch. He was always friendly and polite to her, sometimes striking up a conversation, other times simply giving her a friendly wave if the Jolly Jack was busy. It had gotten so that she looked for him. Even as she approached him now, her pulse did a merry dance when his eyes met hers, her mouth tipping up into a smile.

"There you are," she said as she sat the food in front of him.

He leaned back to allow for the food to be put on the table. "How are you today? It seems quieter in here than usual."

"Very well, Mr Milford. And it's been busy earlier. You got here just in time – that's the last of today's stew."

"Then I must've done something right in my life."

She thought about James's pointed look at Finney's funeral. Not for the first time, she wondered if Seth had been the generous benefactor for that day.

"I hear you're quite the performer these days," he nodded his head at John Tanner. "Everyone has been about the girl fiddler at The Jack."

"I'm sure the shine will wear off eventually," she replied with a smile. "Enjoy your meal, Mr Milford." She turned away, but curiosity poked at her, and she stopped. She looked back, questioning puzzlement on her face. "Are you the one who paid for Finney's funeral? "

"Why, what did you hear?" His tone was neutral, even a little bit amused, but gave nothing away.

"Nothing," she admitted. "No one is saying anything other than it was paid for by somebody local."

Seth shrugged and collected up his spoon, his attention on his food. "I don't know anything about it, either."

Ella watched him for a few seconds, before she said, "You must be a good card player, Mr Milford."

He paused, his spoon halfway to his mouth. "Pardon?"

Ella folded her arms. "My father called it a 'Poker Face'. I can't tell if you're lying or not."

He laughed at that, a rich sound that made her mouth twitch in response. "Well, your father sounded like a fun fellow to know."

"He was."

Her smile was soft and sad. She wasn't sure what her father would think about her working in the dockland's pub, let alone playing the fiddle for several nights already.

"You know, Ella," Seth began then fell silent. His hesitation drew her attention. He was always so calm and confident, and now, if anything he looked a little gauche.

"Yes?"

"Would you please do me the honour of allowing me to accompany you on a walk?"

Of all the things Ella thought he was going to say, that was not it. She blinked at him for a moment.

"Please?"

As she studied his face, a myriad of reasons about why she shouldn't ran through her mind. Her spontaneous response was to say no. She was too busy. She was supposed to be keeping a low profile, although the longer the time passed, the safer she was beginning to feel. Seth Milford was respected and very well-liked throughout the Docklands. Even her uncle seemed to like him. He was very handsome and must be wealthy, judging by the quality of his clothing, yet ate in a public house every day.

Ella gave him a tentative smile. "I'm off on Friday afternoon if that would suit you."

Seth grinned at her, and her stomach did a slow roll. "That would suit me just fine, he replied.

CHAPTER 22

 eth

USUALLY, Seth was confident in any social situation.

He spent his life negotiating business contracts and dealing with all walks of life, from the most recalcitrant captain down to the lowliest of dockworkers. And yet he felt as nervous as a boy on his first day at a new school.

He'd conversed with a range of women, of course, but usually, they were being chaperoned to ensure that the proper social rules were being followed. As Seth and Ella strolled along the sun-dappled paths of the park in the centre of their glorious city, he felt a newfound sense of freedom. Seth couldn't help but feel charmed by Ella's lively conversation, her sparkling blue eyes alight with passion as they discussed the politics of the day.

He'd collected her in his carriage away from The Jolly Jack – at her insistence, though it suited him, too. The last thing he needed was for someone to mention this meeting to his father. Her navy dress contrasted with her skin, and she'd worn her dark hair up. The knowledge that she'd made an effort for him fed into his ego, and he didn't mind admitting it.

May had continued to bless them with her sunshine. Parasols bobbed about the park though Ella didn't seem all that concerned that she was without one. She was keener to engage in their conversation. She was well versed on the women's vote, and how Gladstone had inserted himself back into office. Her passionate voice rang out through the peaceful park, causing a few passers-by to pause and listen in. But Seth didn't mind. He was enthralled by Ella's intellect and the way she could articulate her thoughts so clearly.

She spoke well about a variety of subjects and her father was prominent in most of her stories. The melancholy that he could sense in her whenever she spoke about him told him that there was more to the story, but he didn't want to pry and ruin their happy mood. He preferred it when he could make her laugh.

She stopped on a stone bridge that spanned one of the streams to watch a row of ducklings follow their mother through the water. Seth couldn't take his eyes off her. Her serene smile, the way the curls framed her pretty face, the sweep of her dark lashes where they met high cheekbones. If she was aware of his staring, she didn't show it, though she met his avid gaze just once before she carried on walking.

"Do you often walk through here?"

Seth shook his head. "I rarely have time off, if I'm honest. We have ships all around the world. They arrive in port at different times, often dependent on tides and weather."

"I should like to travel one day," she mused.

"Have you ever left the country?"

She shook her head. "My father worked in London, of course, but his business took him all over the place. He travelled abroad a lot with work, more so when I was older."

"What did he do?"

"He was a solicitor, but his work was more heavily influenced by the commercial side of the law."

"It sounds as though you were close to him."

Ella's eyes tracked the treeline, her lips compressing into an unhappy line. "Yes, very, though not so much in recent years."

Seth saw the underlying anger shimmer in her eyes, and was hit with a hundred more questions, but was unwilling to continue down this line of questioning as she was clearly uncomfortable.

Other couples were walking through the park, following the figure-of-eight path that weaved through the trees and past the lake. Between the flowerbeds and the bushes, babbling streams sparkled in the sunlight as they flowed into the lake.

As they neared the ornate iron bandstand, a new addition to the park, Seth's attention was drawn to the intricate details of the structure. "Have you ever seen anything like it, Ella?" He asked, gesturing toward the structure.

"It is truly magnificent," Ella replied, her gaze fixed on the ornate design. "I read that they are putting these in every town around the country. I should like to see an octagonal one sometime. How engineers must calculate the angles and then meld them together so seamlessly... I mean, the underground train is another wonder to my mind. To tunnel underneath where we stand... it's mind-blowing, don't you agree?"

"I do."

The conversation moved on, as they walked through the park, turning from the political climate to his business. She listened intently as he shared his opinions on the changes that were happening as companies struggle to move from timber to steam. And the changes that were being made to the trade laws around the globe.

"Ships are getting bigger and faster," Seth told her. "Which is fantastic. We can move products much more expediently. My father is keen for bigger, for better."

"And you're not?"

"The problem comes when a ship runs into trouble. We had one that was damaged when it was caught in a storm. It was damaged by rocks. The new metal double hull meant that it stayed afloat, so we were able to salvage the stock and more importantly, no lives were lost. But repairing it was, well, it was a nightmare."

"How so?"

"Because there are not many docks in the world that are big enough to deal with the kind of boats my father is investing in. We had to take the ship out of commission for much longer because it had to be taken to Liverpool. They are the only port in the world with dry docks big enough to take it out of the water for the repairs to be made."

She stopped; her brow furrowed. "Surely, it makes more economic sense to have a higher quantity of smaller boats that can be repaired easily. How much business did you lose whilst waiting for that bigger one to be repaired?"

Seth smiled at her words, feeling a sense of pride at her astute observations. "More than enough."

"Can't you make the changes to the business yourself?"

"Unfortunately," he replied, "my father is a stickler for doing things the way he's always done them. He was amongst the first to move to steamboats - it was against the grain then, and the vessels have gotten bigger and better. I've tried to reason with him to wait for the dockyards around the world to catch up, but he won't have it."

"Then that's a shame that he doesn't have your foresight," she said.

Seth chuckled, delighted that he should have her

support. However, it was her intellect that he found most charming. She could hold her own in a conversation such as this had him wondering about her upbringing, about the man who'd raised her. "Did you speak about business with your father?"

"Not so much once Thomas got older."

Seth pulled up short. "Who's Thomas?"

Seth could tell that she'd regretted her words as soon as he caught her pained expression. He wanted to retract the question, to ease the disquiet that rolled off her. He wanted to go back to their easy conversation, for the spirited woman to come back to him.

She cleared her throat gently, her eyes moving about the scenery beyond his shoulders. "He was my brother."

He was my brother.

Had he died with his father? Seth waited for her to say more but she seemed to slide deep into thought. There was time to explore the matter later for he intended on getting to know her better.

"I'm sorry," Seth said. "We can talk about something else. How about we go and get an ice cream? There's usually a barrow selling one at the park gates?"

Her smile was stiff, and she negated her head. "Perhaps later."

"Very well."

They resumed walking, his mind searching for something – for anything – that would bring her smile back and end the silence that stretched between them.

"Should I take you back?"

Her blue eyes swam with emotion. "Am I boring you already?"

The sass pulled a reluctant chuckle from him. "Golly, no. Far from it."

"Speaking about my father is a subject that brings me pain," she admitted. "He died suddenly, and very unexpectedly. My brother, Thomas," the name was spoken scathingly, "he stayed with his mother. His mother doesn't like me very much. She never has. And that's all I wish to say about the matter, so can we talk about something else?"

His fingers ached to touch her, to kiss her until the anguish that creased her face was replaced with something much more elemental. The rush of images that filled him almost took his breath. He had to clear his throat before he trusted his voice. "We can speak about whatever you wish."

So, they did. They found a bench and sat down, continuing their discussion as they watched the world go by. Seth felt a sense of contentment wash over him, listening to her speak with such conviction. She grew passionate about musical tastes and made him laugh with her outspoken quips.

As the sun slid towards the horizon, he knew that this was just the beginning of their journey together. But for now, at this moment, he was perfectly content to sit with this pretty girl by his side, basking in the warm sunshine and the beauty of the park.

lsie

ELSIE DUFFY CONSIDERED herself one of the lucky ones.

Her mother had earned her coin the same as most women at the docks. Elsie's flame-red hair and green eyes hinted at her Irish blood, though Kate Duffy wouldn't have known which Irish sailor fathered her daughter.

Elsie had known from a young age that she hadn't wanted to live the same as her mother did. Waking up in the doss house, or worse, seeking out the next rough boatman who'd pay her with whisky and a smile.

Elsie had worked hard to steer away from that life, though the docks were where she'd always felt the most comfortable. She'd sold fresh rocket and wreaths alongside the costermongers when she was tiny. She'd learned to weave nets and had washed pots at many of the taverns. Maud Tomlinson was an old crow, but underneath that hard exterior, Elsie knew that a good woman lurked there.

James and Maud didn't have any children, so when Elsie had cheekily knocked on the door, Maud had chased the skinny little girl off her stoop, after she'd handed her bread and cheese. Day after day, Elsie returned until Maud had succumbed to the spirited girl.

One day, Elsie hoped to own a public house of her own. The people who drank here were just as much family as the Tomlinsons were and she lived the camaraderie here. Ever since Ella had arrived, Elsie had felt a kinship to the girl, though she knew that someone with as much class as Ella did wouldn't be around the docklands for very long, especially not when she was spending the afternoon with the handsome Milford.

Elsie slipped through the hatch, a ready smile on her face for the man who'd just ducked in through the door of the Jolly Jack. Experience told her that he wasn't a local, nor was he a docker. He was tall and broad, with jet-black hair slicked close to his skull. The scar that sliced his brow gave him a slight squint.

"What can I get you?"

"Ale," he said, his eyes roaming the bar, towards the door behind her. He put a coin on the bar.

Elsie unhooked a tankard from above her head and began pulling on the beer engine so that the liquid fizzed in the glass bottom. Not a stevedore – maybe military, she surmised. "What brings you to London?"

"Are you here alone?"

Her brow quirked as she put the pint in front of him, her friendly smile in place, though it no longer reached her eyes. There was something off about him. "I'm in a public house," she gestured behind him.

"I'm looking for someone," he muttered, eyes slowly tracking the crowd.

Elsie swiped up the coin as apprehension slithered through her blood. "Do you have a name? Maybe I can help you."

The man's eyes moved back to hers, his eyes flat. He picked up the pint and drained the glass. Elsie could see that his left hand was scarred, too. She'd lay her weeks wages that it was a knife that had done the damage. The glass was banged onto the bar.

He wiped his mouth with his fingers. "Elizabeth Tomlinson."

Elsie kept her face passive. "Can't say as I know anyone by that name."

The man's eyes narrowed. "A Tomlinson owns this place, doesn't he?"

Elsie picked up a cloth and wiped up the ring of moisture left by his glass and then she dipped his glass in the bucket under the bar and dried it. "That's right."

The man sighed deeply, frustrated when she didn't offer any more explanation. He reached into his pocket and dropped a banknote onto the bar top. "Any information you have will help."

Elsie's green gaze turned flinty. The ten-pound note was more than she'd make in half a year. "I don't know an Elizabeth Tomlinson."

"How about an Ella Tomlinson?"

Elizabeth was often shortened to other names. It only stood to reason that Ella's proper name was Elizabeth. She carefully hung the pint glass back up and then leaned onto the bar. This time, she let her annoyance flash in her face. "The landlord has a niece called Ella."

His mouth lifted and he slid the note closer to her. Elsie watched the action and lifted her gaze back up.

"What do you want with her?"

"That's none of your concern."

Elsie straightened up, nonchalantly looking behind him. Ella was out for the afternoon. She didn't know for the life of her what this man wanted with her, but it couldn't be good. Ella had shown up here, out of the blue, like a frightened little mouse who feared its own shadow.

"You're too late," she told him.

"What?"

"She was here but that was weeks ago."

She could tell that he'd not expected the news. "Where did she go?"

Elsie shrugged and then folded her arms. Predictably, his gaze dropped to her chest, then back to her face. "I'm not the girl's keeper. She turned up here, all spoiled. She pestered her uncle for money and then left to go north."

"Where?"

"Leeds, wasn't it?" The gruff voice pulled the stranger's gaze around. At that moment, she could have kissed Seamus O'Flanagan. The twin brothers had been listening in.

Elsie clicked her fingers and nodded. "That's right, Seamus." She angled a look at the man and smiled broadly. "She went to Leeds."

The man considered the three of them. "I'll be back if you're lying."

Elsie plucked the note off the bar and tucked it into her bosom. "And I'll be here waiting, sweetheart."

CHAPTER 24

lla

"WHERE IS ELSIE TONIGHT?" Seamus O'Flanagan slurred from across the bar, his eyelids at half-mast.

Ella chuckled. "For the tenth time tonight, Seamus, Elsie is sick in her bed."

Seamus's head fell forward. His sandy hair had lightened with age, though it was long and tangled as it fell across his face. "I'd take care of her. I'd look after her really well."

Last orders had been called and Ella had done her best to see everybody out.

Mickey, Seamus's older brother by half an hour, was staring at his brother as if he'd lost his mind. He shook his head and lifted his tankard to his lips. "Give it up man. A girl like Elsie would never marry the likes of you, no matter how many times you ask her."

"I'll ask her 'til the end of time," Seamus mumbled, "and when I'm a ghost, I'll follow her and tell her sweet nothings in her ear like the winds whispering through the ribbons tied to a tree."

Mickey stared at his brother. "You bumblin' eejit. What are you going on about?"

Ella flattened her palm on the bar and leaned over, peering into Mickey's tankard. "You know, my uncle won't get rich if you sip at that like a little bird all night. Finish up and get back to the doss house, ya wee dolt." She added the last part in a mock Irish accent.

Mickey sent her a pained look. "I remember when you were a kind and timid girl who wouldn't say boo to a goose. Now you're just mean."

She caught the movement in the corner of her eye as Seth pressed to his feet, but she gave him a slight shake of her head. The O'Flanagan brothers were harmless and as part of the furniture as the chairs that they sat on. They spent a lot of coins in the bar and had hearts of gold, even if they didn't know when they'd had their fill of ale.

"I'm not mean, Mickey," she said. "But I am tired. It's been a long day. I've had to run this place by myself all night."

Seamus reared back his head and blinked sleepily at her. "Where is James?"

This time, Ella didn't bother hiding her exasperation. "For the love of Zeus, Seamus. I've told you this already too. Maud's gone to stay with her sister for a few days. James, too."

The fact that they'd left her in charge of The Jolly Jack was both worrying and exciting. He'd said as much to Seth and almost cried with relief when she'd seen his familiar dark head from across the crowded bar earlier that night. She'd not even had to ask him, but he'd made himself available.

"Did you tell me that already?" Mickey's mumbling was cut off as the door burst inwards and a group of rowdy men stumbled in.

Ella cursed her stupidity for not locking the door. They were dressed in rags, their faces filthy from a full day's work. She knew that they were trouble as they were the same group that had been in the Jolly Jack a few nights ago. She wasn't in the mood for any more bother tonight.

She came around the edge of the bar and lifted the hatch. "Sorry, gentlemen, the pub is closed," she said firmly, crossing her arms over her chest.

The men ignored her and headed straight for the empty bar. Their numbers were too many for the O'Flanagan brothers to stop as they leaned across the bar top to grab at the bottles. Seth tried to reason with them, but they were too drunk to listen.

One of them knocked over a glass, and it shattered on the floor, causing the others to burst out laughing. Without hesitation, Ella grabbed the broom and swung it in the air, letting out a loud yell.

"I said the pub is closed," she repeated, her voice firm and steady.

"Come on, woman!" One whined, turning back to the bar. "All we want is a drink–"

"I don't care if you want holy blessings!" She yelled at them and shook the broom, advancing on the group. "Do I need to get a constable in here? Or a superintendent? Get home, the lot of you! The. Place. Is. Closed!" She stated the words succinctly, bellowing the last syllable to make her point.

The man exchanged looks and they relented, stumbling out through the door. Ella sent another glare across the room at the O'Flanagan Brothers. Mickey, the soberest of the two, grabbed his brother and shuffled passed her, bidding her a bashful goodnight.

Ella slammed the door shut and sent home the three bolts before she leaned against it and let out of whoosh of breath. Seth was standing in the centre of the room, his eyes shining bright. For a moment, he simply stared before he burst into laughter.

"What is it?"

"I'm not saying the word whilst you're standing there with a weapon," Seth chortled.

Ella shifted away from the door and set the broom against the wall. "I don't care to be laughed at," she muttered as she walked past him, but Seth's hand snaked out and caught hold of her wrist, pulling her back around to face him.

"I'm laughing at them, Ella," he murmured. "All those

187

big strapping men running away from a young girl, waggling a broom at them. Did you ever picture yourself doing such a thing when you first arrived here?"

Memories of the first time that she'd ever set eyes on Seth Milford flooded back. That day, she'd been filled with abject terror as the odorous man had grabbed her. Tonight, she'd just chased a crowd of thugs out of her uncle's bar in case they did more damage.

Her answering smile was just as quick and fast as the bubble of laughter that escaped her. "No, I never did."

"You should be proud of yourself," Seth said, the light from the oil lamps making his eyes dance with the mirth reflected in them. "Running a tavern like this one is no mean feat."

A satisfied smile slid across her mouth. She knew that working in a public house in the docklands could be dangerous work. Thievery and prostitution were a part of her day so much that it didn't bother her, as long as the thieves didn't take anything of hers and the *dollymops* stayed out of the pub. Everyone had to survive. "The Jolly Jack has saved me, in more ways than one," she said. "I owe my aunt and uncle a lot, so I did it for them."

"That O'Flanagan was right, Ella. You've come a long way from the timid girl who first stepped in here. I'm very glad we met."

"I should clean up the broken glass and close up," she said, her dry throat making her voice raspy.

His eyes dwelt on her lips as she spoke. Ella felt her breath catch in her throat as she met the need in his gaze with a desire of her own.

Seth's eyes traced her face and he slowly closed the gap between them. In the silence of the bar, she became aware that the air around them shifted into something more. Her heartbeats quickened as Seth closed the gap further still, his fingers linking with hers. Where their skin touched was hot and feverish, sending her blood roaring through her ears.

Her gaze fell to his mouth, her tongue sneaking out to moisten her lips. Those obsidian eyes of his tracked the movement, and his hand came up to cup her cheek. His thumb feathered slowly across her bottom lip, and then his hand slid around to cup her head as he closed the gap between them completely.

Her eyes drifted closed, and her head fell back as Seth feathered tiny little kisses around the edge of her lips as if seeking permission. In answer, Ella turned so that their mouths met, and she surrendered herself to his touch.

CHAPTER 25

*E*lla placed a fiddle back in its box and snapped the brass locks into place after she'd shut the lid.

"You know, you could probably afford to get yourself a newer one of those now."

Startled, she gave her uncle a sharp look as she petted the case. "No! I couldn't do that to Finney."

James chuckled as he locked the door to the Jolly Jack and made his way back behind the bar. The air was still thick with smoke, a heavy mixture of tobacco and wood. It had been a busy night with sailors and merchants filling the place.

"I'm not sure if you noticed but there were new faces in here tonight."

Ella shook her head. Once she got into the music, she barely noticed anyone in the room. "That's good to know, though I'm not sure how sensible it is. I'm supposed to be keeping a low profile."

"It's been months, Ella. Clara would have made her move before this if she was going to. She's bound to have married that doctor by now."

Her heart tripped about in her ribcage. "Have you heard?"

"No, and I don't pay any mind to the papers. Would such a story be newsworthy? I doubt it."

Her feet were aching after a long day, and she pulled up a stool next to the bar. She'd tried to push Clara out of her mind. It had been easier recently since she'd picked up the fiddle, in fact. She felt as if she'd finally found where she fit into her new life.

"Looks like we had a good night," James said, his eyes sparkling with excitement as he was starting to count the night's earnings.

"Aye, we did," Ella replied, stifling a yawn. "But I'm ready for bed."

James chuckled. "You're too young to be tired, girl."

"My feet are telling me a different story."

Elsie had cleared most of the glasses before she left. As Ella looked around the room, she could see that there was still more work to be done before she could finish for the night. Light from the oil lamps danced across the whitewash walls, reflecting off the brass fittings, and the polished wood of the bar.

"We'll have to restock the ale in the morning," James noted. "Will you go to the brewery when you're up and ask for two extra kegs?"

Elena nodded in agreement; her eyes fixed on the door. She wondered if Seth would come in, but she

ANNIE SHIELDS

knew it was unlikely. A man like him shouldn't be spending time in a place such as this, especially with someone like her.

James followed her gaze to the door. "He's not coming by tonight, Ella. You know that."

Sometimes, Seth would be at the public house if he knew that she was going to be playing her fiddle, but tonight's effort had been an impromptu event. She'd been cajoled into just one song but that was never enough for her, and she'd played all night.

Ella sighed and looked down at her hands, her fingers tracing the grain of the wood along the bar top. "I know, Uncle James. It's just…"

"You're in love with him," James finished for her. His eyes shone with sympathy when she looked up. "Maud and I have both seen how you are together but you…" He set down the coins he'd been sorting and placed his hands on the edge of the bar. He looked at her in earnest. "You must know that he comes from a different world than ours. Now that your father isn't here, I feel it's fallen to me to be the one to keep an eye out for you. His father is the type that would never like him to be with a girl like you."

Ella knew this to be true, but it didn't make that ache in her heart any less painful. She nodded and looked down. He'd only kissed her once, that night weeks ago, but there hadn't been much time spent together since. He'd been called north to tend to the shipments using various docks, or he'd been at their country estate.

192

James reached across the bar and squeezed her shoulder gently. "You'll find the right man one day. Of course, he'll have to get through me first."

A watery smile wobbled across her mouth. She was touched by his sentiment. "I do wish my father was here. I wish that you could have settled your differences properly, face to face."

James' hand fell to the bar with a heartfelt sigh, his mouth twisting ruefully. "Your sentiment echoes my own, Ella." He took two stubby glasses and filled each of them with whisky, pushing one toward her. "Let's drink to your father."

Ella lifted her glass, the action mirroring James'.

"To you, Henry, you old goat."

"To Papa," she whispered, taking a deep swallow of the fiery amber liquid. She grimaced at her uncle's gleeful expression after he'd drained the glass and set it down with a flourish. His lips peeled back, and he exhaled noisily. "Enough to put hairs on your chest, girl."

She set the glass down, unsure how men could drink the stuff neat. "It's revolting."

James sniggered and snatched up her glass, too. "Just like your father. His taste was always more refined, too."

"He drank. He drank a lot towards the end," Ella said.

He eyed her over the rim of the glass. "Your father?"

She gave a small nod. "They argued a lot. He tried to

hide it but Clara… she had a way of emasculating him without yelling."

James finished her whisky, poured himself another and set the bottle down with a bang. "I tried to warn that stubborn idiot."

"What do you mean?"

"When you told me that Clara was in cahoots with the doctor, well, I wasn't in the least bit surprised. It's not the first time she's shown affection to another man. Your father had an ambitious young man called Matthew Allerton who joined the firm. Charming as you like, and confident with it."

Ella frowned as the name tickled out a familiar memory, but she remained silent, and James continued. "I caught Clara in his arms. Matthew was handsome, but he didn't have Henry's wealth. Clara was still affianced to your father then. Henry refused to believe me. Matthew was fired and cut out of Henry's life and Clara…" James sighed and drank again. "She turned him against me. I'd bought the Jolly Jack with my share of the inheritance we'd received from our father. I imagine that Clara had made him look at ways at blocking me from getting that money.

Maud had just lost another child – a boy," James was staring into the glass as if it held all the secrets of the past. His voice was rough and low, with pain etched into the groves that bracketed his mouth. "It was a dark time for us both. I needed my brother. You were still so young. I turned up at his house. I was drunk, of course, but it was our third child that had died.

Henry told me that he couldn't afford to have his business blackened by a dockland's tavern. He threw me out and refused to take any more visits. He wouldn't reply to my letters.

I was a liar. Now I was a drunkard."

James straightened up and she caught the look of conflicted emotion there. "When you arrived here, I thought about that night. The last time I'd seen him. I wonder now if his anger was simply embarrassment on his part. Clara was there and she was furious that I'd caused a scene in the street." He held the glass up, inspecting the contents as he rotated the glass in his hand. "You could have knocked me down with a feather when his letter arrived. I almost burned it, but Maud stopped me. She reminded me that I was not the man they'd made me out to be."

"I'm glad she did that," Ella's said tenderly. "I don't know where I'd be now if Papa hadn't mentioned your name, or if I hadn't discovered your letters."

"It's like salt in a wound to know how he died. Do you think she poisoned him?"

"I move between both, but I have no proof either way. I just know that whatever affliction ailed my father in those last months? That last night he'd been just fine at dinner."

"Would your cook be open to bribes?"

Ella gave a deliberate shake of her head. "No. The staff were loyal to my father. But Clara would come down when there was a dinner party and interfere. It drove Cook barmy but she couldn't say anything as

Papa always sided with Clara and she was the mistress of the house."

James pursed his lips and then drank the contents of his glass. "We might not be able to do anything, but her Judgement Day will come."

"It's a shame we won't get front-row seats," Ella added mutinously.

James laughed then, a deep rich sound. "Every so often, Ella Tomlinson, your mother comes flying out of your mouth."

A warm sense of happiness washed over her. "Papa said that sometimes. I don't remember her, but I wish I did."

"Oh, your father loved her. I think it drove Clara insane knowing that she could never fill her shoes. Your father never let his love for your mother go out. Clara hated competing with her ghost."

Ella nodded, recalling vividly the snippy words that she'd overheard from her stepmother's mouth, and Henry begging her to refrain from saying such spite when Ella was around.

"I think you being here is Henry's way of trying to heal our rift. He apologised in one of his letters, about being callous over the death of my son."

Ella remembered the heartfelt response that James had written. She'd had to fill in the blanks because she only had James' side of the replies, but she'd guessed right when she'd surmised that her uncle had lost a child. It was so commonplace, but it still didn't ease the pain of such a loss.

"So many years of bad blood, so much wasted time." His voice grew quieter with each syllable. James took a moment before he inhaled sharply and shook his head. "Maud tells me whisky makes me mawkish."

"It's fine to miss your brother," Ella said. "I miss Thomas even though he's not really my kin."

James' face twisted with cynicism. He snatched up the glasses and dipped them in the bucket to rinse them. "You grew up thinking that boy was your brother. When that space in your life is no longer occupied, it leaves a void. Of course, you miss him, but he's Clara's boy. And, knowing Clara the way we do, the boy will be fine."

"She does love her son. That's her one saving grace," Ella added.

James looked at her then, as though surprised that she could still offer kindness to Clara's character. "If my own children had lived, I wish they'd have been like you. You're like a daughter to me."

She smiled, her sense of belonging warming her. "Thank you, uncle. Truly."

He set the glasses on the bar, upside down to dry. "You know, one of these days, you'll be leaving me behind."

Ella folded her arms along the top of the bar. "That won't happen."

"Yes, it will. You'll be on stage at the Old Mo on Drury Lane, performing for the rich and famous. You'll have better men than Seth Milford falling at your feet, and you'll talk about that dingy old bar in the dockyard with that fuddy old uncle of yours. And I'll be stooped over and blind," James bent over and shuffled along, squinting his eyes.

Ella laughed. Her heart squeezed at the thought of having Seth openly declare his love for her. It was a dream to live in a world where love would be enough to bridge the gap between their worlds. She was honest enough with herself to know that her talent was never good enough for one of the popular music halls and that her dreams would vanish like the mists off the river when the sun rose.

"Honestly, Uncle, you should be on stage, too."

He straightened up, pushing his hair back off his face as he did. "No, my girl. You are the one they're calling the Darling of the Dockyard. But darling or not, those glasses won't clean themselves."

Lips twitching, Ella hopped down off her stool and helped her uncle clean up.

CHAPTER 26

"Driver!" Seth rapped sharply on the roof of the carriage. It came to a halt, the shouts of the driver muffled as he called to his horses. The carriage rocked and she could hear the rattle of the iron-shod hooves against the street.

Ella looked through the window. Seeing the familiar thoroughfare view beyond it filled her with disappointment. It was the same street where he'd met her earlier that day. The same one where their rendezvous always happened.

The day had started with such promise but ever since James had pointed out the differences in their social status and how it would never work between them, Ella had grown ever watchful of the little things Seth did, like stopping the carriage far enough away from the docks so that they wouldn't be seen together by anyone that knew him.

He turned in his seat and let out a little sigh. "Thank you for such a lovely afternoon."

She blinked rapidly, turning to look out of the window. She'd been so excited to see him. She'd had a dress made, paid for out of the earnings she'd made playing her fiddle. The grey colour suited her skin tone and fitted her form neatly. She'd carefully arranged her dark hair so that she would look the part on the arm of such a fine gentleman as Seth Milford. She'd been rewarded by his look of appreciation when he'd first seen her. And yet, throughout the afternoon, she'd noticed that his eyes were ever watchful of the crowds around them. James' words of warning about a dalliance with Seth slithered through her happiness, and she noticed Seth's actions even more.

She didn't want to cry in front of him but her eyes watered, nonetheless.

He reached for her hand. "What's the matter?"

She had to swallow twice for the constriction of emotion in her throat to ease enough for her to be able to speak. "My uncle was right about you, that's all."

She risked a look at him. His dark brow furrowed. "What about?"

"You're afraid to be seen with me," she said, her voice barely above a whisper. "You're ashamed of me."

She looked across the space at him, daring him to deny it, but his pained expression confirmed her fears. The cabby tapped the side of the carriage to let them know that he was waiting. Ella moved to open the door, but Seth stopped her.

"Ella, wait. It's not that I'm ashamed of you. It's just that my family is traditional and has certain expectations."

"Expectations that I can't possibly meet," Ella said, bitterness creeping into her voice.

Seth reached out to take her hand, but she snatched it back, shrinking back against the side of the carriage. "Don't, Seth."

Seth looked away; his face clouded with uncertainty. "It's complicated, Ella."

"Not for me it isn't."

His brow hooked up. "Really?"

She blinked at the sarcastic tone. "What does that mean?"

He folded his arms, a challenging light igniting those obsidian eyes of his. "I know nothing about your life before you arrived at The Jolly Jack, Ella. Nothing about where you came from. Every time I steer the conversation to something remotely personal about your past, your response is to remind me that our time is short, and we ought to find a more interesting subject."

Her jaw snapped shut and she rolled her lips inwards, her heart lurching in her chest. He was right. She'd kept her painful past hidden because she was afraid that it might change how he viewed her. Her father had died penniless, killed by his wife. Who would want to risk that level of scandal, especially when it would adversely affect his business here in England?

The silence pulsed with tension. The cabby tapped the side of the hansom again and Ella bellowed, "Just a minute!"

Seth rubbed at the spot between his brows, his sigh puncturing the air. "You don't understand the pressures I'm under. The demands of not just my family, but also my peers, my colleagues..."

"Do I make you happy?"

His expression softened and he nodded. "Very."

She searched his face, longing for him to assure her that what he said was true, that it would somehow be enough for them both, but she knew that it never would be. She loved him, but even that wouldn't span the chasm that stretched between them. Her gaze moved back through the window.

"Please, let's not ruin a perfectly delightful day by quarrelling."

She turned back to him, forcing a smile. "We're not quarrelling. It's fine."

"I enjoy spending this time with you. My father... is a difficult man. And my work is demanding. I've told you this. I must go where I'm needed for the sake of the company. My grandfather... there is a long history. My mother and my siblings rely on me..."

"It's fine," she repeated, a rush of hurt washing over her. "I understand that you'll never marry beneath your station. I suppose that I shouldn't be surprised."

She reached for the handle. Seth pulled her round to face him, brows knitted together, eyes glittering with anger. "Explain yourself."

Her mutinous body quivered at his touch. Annoyed, she looked down at his hand. He lifted his fingers away from her and prompted her to speak. "You're too afraid to stand up for what you want," Ella replied, her voice cold. "Too afraid to take a risk. Instead, you hide behind your excuses, your society's rules, your fear."

A tremor ran through her as she saw that her barbed words hit home. She'd hurt him. She wanted to take them back, to apologise, to continue to sneak about with him as long as she got to be with him. But when would it end? She knew her father would not have approved of this sneaking about any more than her uncle did. "I'm just a lowly fiddle player who will never be good enough for you."

This time, she unlatched the door, startling the driver who leapt out of the way.

"Ella! Let me get you a cab, at least. It's a long way to the docks from here."

She stepped out onto the street. "I can pay for my own bloody carriage, thank you very much. I don't need your money or your pity."

Seth leaned out of the door. "Will you let me see you again?"

She took a moment to shake out the long skirts of her dress, using the time to compose herself. She wanted to tell him no, but she couldn't bring herself to utter the words. Instead, she gave him a dismissive shrug of her shoulders, walking away safe in the knowledge that he wouldn't follow her in case he was seen with her.

eth

Seth took a deep breath as he stepped into the office of Milford Shipping, his heart is heavy with dread. Charles had already warned him that his father was on the warpath. It seemed ironic to him that as soon as he'd had his first argument with Ella, it seemed that his secret had been blown.

Seth would never know whom it was that had tipped Philip Milford off to the fact that his eldest son had been seen with the same woman on several occasions, but Charles had told him this morning that his father wanted answers.

"How nice of you to join me," Philip intoned, drolly.

Seth took his time hanging up his hat and hooking his cane on the edge of his desk. His father was seated at his desk, papers bunched in his hands, and spread across the surface in front of him. The office was peaceful after most of the clerks had gone home. Even the yard beyond the dusty window had fallen silent for the day. Seth had spent another delightful afternoon with Ella. How he longed to hold onto the joy he always felt in her presence, instead of this cold disquiet.

"Good afternoon, Father," Seth said, trying to sound as casual as possible.

"Where have you been?"

Seth debated lying to the man. "Out enjoying the weather," he said, his mind scrambling for a suitable explanation, even as Ella's words came back to haunt him.

You're too afraid to take a risk.

He'd watched Ella walk away from him, head held high and drawing the eyes of all the men that she passed. He wanted to snatch her back inside the hansom, to gather her close and lay his claim on her, but he had no right. She deserved so much more than sneaking about with the likes of him. Perhaps he should come clean with his father. After all, he reasoned, he took a risk every day that he did business.

Philip looked up from his papers with a stern expression on his face. "Are you going to tell me who was in your carriage with you? You were seen last Friday and again earlier today. I'm guessing that's just where you've come from now, too."

"You are always reminding me that I'm a man of

twenty-seven, Papa." Seth sat down and began to point-lessly shuffle papers around.

Philip raised an eyebrow. "Seth."

Seth hesitated for a moment. He knew that his father wouldn't approve of Ella, with her lower social, standing, and outspoken views on women's rights. "Just a friend."

Philip fixed him with a steely gaze. "I see. And who might that friend be?"

"It's not important." The last thing he wanted to do was admit to his father that he'd fallen in love with a barmaid. The news that his future daughter-in-law played a fiddle in a dockyard public house would prob-ably be enough to finish his father off and send his mother to the asylum. "How come you're here so late?"

"It's a good job I am considering my son is taking so much time off."

Seth resisted the urge to roll his eyes. "I'm still getting all the work done, Father. You do not need to worry."

"On the contrary. The talk I'm hearing is that you're spending a lot of time with this *friend*. My point is, if I've heard about it, then there's nothing to stop it from getting whispered into Harrison's ears."

Seth shifted uncomfortably. "I am not engaged to his daughter so what does it matter."

"*Yet*," Philip stressed the word with a look. "And it matters because we are going to need Harrison's money. That boat being fixed has hurt the cash flow."

"I told you this would happen," Seth said.

"I don't want to hear it," Philip shouted. "Seth, I was young once, too. I sowed my fair share of wild oats, my boy. But I also knew that I had a duty to my father's business, to his reputation, just as you have to this one. You can have all the fun you want once you're married. You're just not being at all discreet about meeting up with this tart."

Seth shot to his feet. "She is no such thing!"

Philip sat back, expression thoughtful, as his fingers tapped on the edges of the papers in his hand. Seth slowly lowered himself back into his chair, knowing that he'd overplayed his hand. He couldn't help but feel resentful towards his father. He was tired of being put into situations that he didn't want to be in. He was fed up with having to keep up appearances simply to appease his father and maintain his family's reputation.

"This woman, the one in the grey dress," Philip said. "Does she have any means of support?"

Seth kept his face passive, even with the mention of Ella's new dress colour. His father's spies had been thorough, at least. He realised that he didn't know if she had an income from her father's death. Everything that he'd said to her in the cab had been true. It annoyed him that she'd remained so tight-lipped about her past and that he knew very little about her.

He hadn't meant to blurt it out in an argument the way he had but she'd put him on the spot, and he'd been like a child pointing out her flaws instead of answering to his own.

He had intended on doing a little digging into her

past but had been having far too much fun getting to know her that he'd not done his investigating. He shook his head, knowing that his father was thinking that Ella was only interested in him for his financial status.

"I don't want you getting involved with someone who could tarnish our family's reputation. If what I'm being told about this woman is true, then she is not the right one for you."

Despair filled him. He longed to explain that he cared deeply for Ella, that she wasn't just some distraction for him. He knew that if his father took the time, he too would find Ella kind and intelligent. But telling Philip Milford that a woman wasn't interested in him for his money would be like telling the sun not to rise. So, he remained silent.

Philip continued. "Your mother is expecting us at Linton House this weekend. And you know how important it is to keep up appearances in this line of work."

"Father, I really don't think that–"

Philip cut him off. "You don't have a choice, Seth. You'll be at the house this weekend." It was a command rather than a request. "You will be polite and civil to the Harrison girl and do what it takes to save this company.

And you will end things with this barmaid or, so help me God, I will come down on you like a ton of bricks. I will find out exactly who she is, and I will ruin her life."

Seth met Philip's wrathful gaze, meeting fire with fire. There was no doubt in his mind that his father wouldn't carry out his threat. He didn't know much about Ella's past life, but he knew it had already been filled with much pain. He couldn't be responsible for anything more happening to her. But could he walk away from her? At that very moment, Seth had never hated his father more.

CHAPTER 28

 lla

ELLA WEAVED her way through the bustling streets of London. Overhead, not a cloud marred the cerulean sky and the sun beat down on her back as the heat of July blazed. The warm breeze carried with it the scent of salt and tar, mixed with the sweet aroma of fresh fruit and pies touted by the costermongers who lined the street corners.

She spied the familiar spikes of masts on the horizon as she made her way back toward the docklands.

Men in top hats and waistcoats hurried past her, clutching briefcases and bundles of papers. Workers in dirty overalls pushed carts of cargo down the cobbled streets, grunting and sweating under the weight of their loads.

As she got closer to the docks, the familiar pungent smell of seaweed and fish wafted over her and she could see the river twinkling under the sunlight, the ripples changing as boats sliced through the water. The ones that were moored creaked gently in the wake. The streets were a frenzy of activity, with merchants and traders hurrying between warehouses and ships, sailors hauling their cargo, and horses and carriages jostling for space on the narrow streets, the carts clattering under their weight.

Ella's attention was caught by a group of sailors gathered around a street performer, his juggling and acrobatic skills drawing a large crowd. She smiled as she heard their laughter and applause, her heart swelling with a sense of community and camaraderie.

"'Ere! There she is! The dockyard darlin'!" One of the sailors was pointing at her. "Give us a tune, miss!"

She pointed to her basket. "I don't have my fiddle, I'm afraid!" She laughed at the collective groan, and she blushed with pleasure.

She wasn't sure that she'd ever get used to the unofficial title that she'd been given, nor would she get used to being recognised, but performing most nights at the Jolly Jack was not only bringing her notoriety, it was also filling her uncle's coffers, too. Most days when she was sent to fetch ingredients for the kitchen, she was stopped by several people to speak about her fiddle playing.

James had told Maud to stop bothering Ella with such inconsequential matters, that they could find a boy to help with the tasks, but the truth was that Ella enjoyed it. It also allowed her to walk past Milford Shipping offices.

It had been weeks since she'd seen Seth last. No word of his welfare. No lunchtime visits. She'd asked around about him locally but there was no more news forthcoming. The offices looked much the same as she walked by them. At first, she'd worried that he was hurt but her uncle had informed her that Seth's demise would certainly have reached the depths of the Jolly Jack by now.

She just wished that he'd done her the courtesy of letting her know that he'd lost interest.

She waved at the sailors after getting a promise from them that they'd see her later. One had even asked for a kiss in the bargain. She'd laughed gaily, just as she was meant to, and had left them laughing over the playful wink she'd shot them all. Seth might have turned his back on her without a word but other men were suited better to her – and some who were less suited. Why couldn't she find one of those to make her happy instead?

James worried about her welfare with these men, and the attention that her newfound fame was garnering but she didn't mind. In the dazzling sunlight, the men were harmless, and she was always surrounded by people at the Jolly Jack whenever she played. She told her uncle that he was worried for nowt.

As she made her way through the crowds, more people began to stop her to speak about her fiddle playing. A fishmonger praised her performance at the pub the night before, while a captain asked if she would play for his crew on their next voyage. Ella smiled graciously and thanked each person, happy that her music was bringing joy to those around her.

She would play tonight, she decided. Even if the sailors didn't show up. She would dwell in the joy that she brought to others, even if Seth had done as she'd feared and moved on.

THE STREETS WERE CROWDED. Couples strolling along hand in hand; traders and street sellers hawking their goods, and scraggly children darting in between legs like rats. He longed to shove them all out of the way.

A huge crowd blocked the path, gawking at a man wearing garish rags and tossing balls in the air whilst his feet danced a jig. He had to press against the shop fronts to squeeze by the group, grimacing when he looked down and saw that the movement had swiped the sooty grime off the glass he'd touched onto his clothing.

He stopped to avoid a skinny dog that hobbled along the scorching cobbles and knocked away the seeking hand of a girl who must have noticed that his pockets were bulging. He gripped her wrist and hissed at her, sending her careening back along into the gutters. With a quick pat to check the contents were still in his pocket, he continued on his way.

The heat was unbearable. Sweat trickled down his spine and his shirt stuck to his back but at least as he made his way down to the docks, there was a slight breeze rolling in off the water.

The place reeked to high heaven of fish guts and filth. He knew that his frustrations were borne out of being led on a merry dance chasing this entity. The girl was like a ghost. He'd heard her name in passing by traders and pirates alike, yet he'd never clapped eyes on her.

He knew now that every time he'd been given a piece of information about her – information he'd paid a premium for from one of the sailors – he'd been fed false information. He wasn't sure if the girl was moving around a lot or if the people that he was paying to tell him where she was were too drunk to know.

His task was to find her, and it had taken him months of traipsing around the country looking for her. For a while, he was convinced she'd left the country aboard a ship. She was married to a miner up in the hills of North Wales. She'd joined a circus. Each time, he was led back here. Only now she had a new name.

He ducked into the doorway of the Jolly Jack and had to give his eyes a moment to adjust to the gloomy interior. The door was propped open to allow air in, and his stomach growled when he was hit by the delicious smell of roasting meat. He should eat. It would give him a valid reason to start up a conversation.

He felt several sets of eyes on him when he stepped in. The attractive barmaid that had sent him to Leeds to look for his quarry wasn't in. Good, at least he wouldn't have to hurt her for sending him on a wild goose chase. A burly-looking dockworker nursed his pint of ale but didn't look up when he took a stool next to him.

"Can I buy you a drink?"

The docker slowly raised an eyebrow and pointed to his glass, "What's that – Scotch mist?"

He laughed, because he was supposed to, although the quip annoyed him. "Never have too much ale in my book."

"What do you want?" The voice was low, and his bloodshot eyes were narrowed.

"Some information, my friend. I can pay," he added, keeping his voice down when he noticed that the stocky man behind the bar was watching him.

"Information?" The docker muttered. "What information?"

"I'm looking for someone. They call her the Dockyard Darling."

"What the hell is a dockyard darling?" The docker picked up his glass and he caught the warning look he'd sent to the man standing behind the bar as he took a long pull at his beer.

He bit back a sigh. Fine, they'd do this the hard way. The barman was stocky with watchful blue eyes. His dark hair was threaded with strands of silver, and he'd tied his long hair back.

"Afternoon," the barman said with a lift of his chin when he met the attentive stare. "What's your pleasure?"

"Brandy, if you have it. And a plate of whatever it is that I can smell."

He was rubbing a glass. He held it up to the light pouring through the bay window and scrutinised it. "Sold out, sorry. No food 'til tomorrow."

"Fine," the man grunted. "Just the brandy then. And perhaps some help."

"What with?"

"I'm looking for someone. A woman," he added when the glass appeared in front of him. He set the pile of coins down and waved a note in the air to emphasise his point.

"Ain't we all," the dockworker muttered.

"Not one I pay," he growled, slapping a hand on the bar to cut off the sniggering. "Her name is Elizabeth Tomlinson, but she goes by the name of Ella."

The barman was good. His movements didn't falter, but the light that burned in his eyes blazed bright blue. He must be the uncle that he'd heard so much about.

James Tomlinson pulled a face and shrugged. "Doesn't ring a bell."

"Aren't you James Tomlinson?"

He slung the rag over his shoulder and laid his palms on the bar. "That's right."

"Then she's your niece. You do know her."

'I have a niece, but I've not seen her in decades, son."

"I know she's here. The dockyard darling," he added with a scathing tone.

A muscle bounced in James' jaw as the two men glared at each other. "What do you want with my niece?"

"I just need to speak to her."

"She's not here."

He toyed with the glass, his gaze moving to the liquid swinging around the inside. "I know that she plays her fiddle here. I'll just wait until she's playing next and then I'll speak to her."

"Your money isn't welcome in here, neither are you. Out you go."

The man considered his quarry carefully. He caught the movement out of the corner of his eyes. Without turning around, he knew that he'd been surrounded by the dockworkers, the sailors and the traders who had all been quietly enjoying their drinks when he'd walked in. Slowly, he picked up his glass, considering the consequences of starting a fight when the odds were not in his favour. He tossed the brandy back and set the empty glass down, grimacing as it blazed a path down his gullet. His boss would not be happy if he caused a scene. Not like this.

"I have a job to do," he said.

James Tomlinson shrugged; his mouth pulled down at the corners. "No one cares. Get out. And stay the hell away from my niece. People go missing all the time around here. I'm sure a face as ugly as yours won't be missed."

He skulked out of the bar, knowing that he wasn't going to get paid until he got the job done. But he was going to have to go back to his boss and admit failure.

CHAPTER 29

lla

"Perhaps I should just go to Clara."

"That's a ridiculous suggestion," Elsie said with an exasperated sigh.

Ella looked to her aunt and uncle for support, but their expressions were equally as horror-struck by her idea. "It would cut the head off the snake, would it not? She knows I'm here. I could tell her I have no interest in spilling her dirty secret to the world. That I'm happy and content now."

"I don't even know your stepmother, but the fact that this hoodlum has been in here again looking for you can only spell trouble," Maud folded her arms across her ample bosom.

"He didn't say why she was looking for me?"

"He only mentioned you by name. Full name," James added.

Ella pulled on her lower lip, puzzled by the whole thing. Why would Clara call her by her given name, instead of the name she was known by? Unless she was covering all bases in case Ella had changed it.

"We know what he looks like now," James said. They were gathered in their sitting room. The sun was melding into the skyline, an inferno of magenta and orange streaking the evening sky. "We can be ready for him."

"Why didn't you tell me that he'd been here before?"

Elsie shrugged and looked at Maud. Her aunt said, "Don't be cross with her. She told your uncle and me. We didn't want to worry you."

"That Clara had sent someone to silence me in case I gave away her dark secret?" Ella muttered, pushing to her feet. She wanted to sit by the window, to watch the boats, to be soothed by the lapping of the river, though her uncle had warned her to stay away from the window. Instead, she hovered in the middle of the room, uncertain.

"James warned the locals to remain vigilant. And, until now, it worked." Maud said.

"We don't think that you should play the fiddle anymore," James said tentatively.

Ella whirled on him, fury twisting her face. "Out of the question."

"Ella," James began.

"No, uncle. Absolutely not. She has already taken so

much from me. She set my violin alight. She made me watch it. It was the one last connection that I had to Papa, and she destroyed it, forcing me to bend to her will.

I thought my love for music would stay buried. But this is my livelihood, now. The Jolly Jack is my home. You and Aunt Maud need the income. No, I refuse to cave into her over-zealous actions. I simply won't allow her to take it away from me. If this man had despicable reasons to seek me out, surely, he wouldn't do it in broad daylight?"

James exchanged a look with Maud, with Elsie, before he said, "I suppose that part hadn't occurred to us."

"Perhaps your Mr Milford will come in," Elsie said, a teasing light in her eyes.

"Hardly," Ella scoffed. She longed to confide in Seth, to tell him the truth. She longed to be held in his arms, but she worried her rash actions has pushed him away. He hadn't been in during the evening since before they'd argued. "Uncle James was right. I wasn't good enough for him."

Maud stood and clucked her tongue, "Then he's a fool."

Ella's brows shot up. "Weren't you the one warning me to stay away from him?"

Maud lifted a shoulder, adding coals to the stove and settling the kettle on it. "You're good enough for anyone, Ella. Don't you forget that."

Ella looked at her uncle who was suddenly interested in the fire, then to Elsie who shrugged. Maud had always been the discordant voice in the household and Ella wasn't sure how to respond to her kindness.

The church bells tolled for six and James, relieved, pushed to his feet. "I need to open the bar up. Why don't you stay up here tonight?" he said to Ella from the doorway.

Dread trickled like ice down her spine, churning her supper queasily in her gut. The terror of knowing that Clara was near her was almost paralyzing. Her uncle's suggestion that she should hide away seemed like the right thing to do. She'd be safer if she was tucked away up here. But could she do that night after night? Could she live in fear once more, after she'd had her taste of freedom moving about the docklands?

Hiding away from what she loved would give Clara exactly what she wanted. Ella strengthened her resolve and shook her head. "No, uncle. I will be down shortly. And if people want me to play tonight, then I'll be ready for that, too. If tonight is my last performance, then so be it."

BUT IT WASN'T her last performance.

The strange man didn't show up. Not that night, not any night. Ella's fear and tension began to ease, as the weeks began to drift by. Instead, it was a different tension that niggled her at night. Seth.

Perhaps she should do as the mysterious man

suggested, and simply wait it out at the Milford Shipping Offices, but fear of a final rejection from Seth kept her away from there. His absence was message enough. He's made his choice. Just as she'd made hers.

The Jolly Jack filled with people, just as it did every night. James was right – folks from all walks of life came to the public house to hear her play. She'd joined forces with a piano player and sometimes a singer, though it was often her voice that could be heard soaring above the strings that came alive under her fingers. Who needed a classy music hall like The Middlesex or Canterbury Music Hall?

She played, treating each night as if it was indeed her last, for her music was all that she had left.

CHAPTER 30

 eth

SETH WAS ALREADY REGRETTING the decision to meet up with his friends for the evening, but his friend Cuthbert had led a decent argument. In theory, it had been months since they'd all been in the same city for any great period. In reality, Cuthbert could never handle his liquor and he was growing more belligerent by the minute.

The air in the gentleman's club was heavy with cigar smoke and the murmurs of conversations, though Cuthbert's nasal twang was carrying across the room. He was starting to draw irritated looks from guests beyond where they were sitting in the corner.

The room was grandly furnished, with a staircase on either side of the room curving to the upper floor where distinguished members could spend the night in one of the luxurious rooms. A fire roared in the hearth, casting a warm glow over the leather armchairs and plush sofa that were clustered around in small groupings.

The mahogany bar at the far end of the room was hidden by members who were enjoying a tipple of brandy, whilst others huddled around small tables, their faces illuminated with the soft light from the gas lamps as they discussed the latest political endeavours. Classic hunting scenes and portraits of founding members peered down from the walls, framed for eternity in gilt wood.

"Cuthbert," Peter Bennet murmured, "You might want to tame it down. I'd like to come back here."

"Peter's right," Freddie Walton added.

Cuthbert waved his tumbler around, the whisky sloshing close to the lip of the crystal glass. "Oh, hush up, fellows. They're just jealous that they've no longer got their youth." He cackled at his own wit, missing the exasperated look that moved around the others. He leaned forward, eyes glassy as he gestured at Seth with his glass. "Let's go somewhere else. You know the best spots to go to."

"I think we should call it a night," Peter said, pushing his empty tumbler onto the circular table that they sat around.

"Rubbish, it's still early! Come on, Seth! You're the man about town, where should we go?"

Thinking it might be easier to get him home once

he was in a carriage, Seth asked, "What do you feel like doing?"

Cuthbert snapped his fingers. "Lydia mentioned this quaint little place. It's the talk of the town!" He surged to his feet, knocking the table so that the glasses tumbled off the sides. The resounding crash silenced the room, but Cuthbert didn't care. He was already weaving his way towards the exit, oblivious to the chaos and scowls he was receiving.

"Go keep an eye on him," Seth said to Peter. Freddie quickly followed, leaving Seth to deal with the pious-looking concierge.

By the time he joined the others outside, they had already found a carriage and were waiting for him at the roadside. The cool night air was a welcome relief after the stuffiness of the club, and he took a moment to enjoy the night breeze. He clambered into the waiting cab, and shut the door, giving a quick tap-tap on the door. The carriage jerked and they filtered into the city traffic.

"Couldn't pick a different club to smash glasses in, could you?" Seth said to an unrepentant Cuthbert. "You know that all our fathers will hear about this from the members."

Cuthbert waved him away like he was a sycophantic waiter. "Papa will cover the damages."

Seth shook his head, looking out of the window. John Wilson would write off Cuthbert's behaviour as the exuberance of youth. Philip Milford would be horrified that his son was entangled in such outrageous antics and Seth knew that another lecture would be coming his way. He'd poured himself into work, finding every reason to be out of the city – away from his father, away from the Harrisons – but mostly away from the temptation of seeing Ella.

He'd been in the north, visiting the Quarry Bank mill, to see the cloth that they shipped coming from the source. He'd seen the new docks being built in Liverpool and followed the barges through Birmingham. His father seemed satisfied enough at his communications when he'd written to him to update his discoveries about where they could make improvements and save money, though Philip was yet to implement any of them.

The city was still hectic, with carriages racing along the darkened streets. The shops might be closed but theatres and music halls came alive at night, filled with thrill seekers and the elite seeking entertainment.

Seth frowned when he realised that they were heading South in the city. "Where are we going?"

"Lydia told Cuthbert about this quaint little place that is the talk of the town," Peter shrugged, conveying a look of *'I tried'* to Seth. "He'd instructed the driver before we could stop him."

Knowing just how bullish his friend could be after alcohol, Seth knew it was pointless to try and argue.

Cuthbert grinned. "The night is still young, Seth. I want music. And there's only one place in the city where we'll get it."

When he recognised the hulk of St. Peter's church, a sense of dread rolled through the pit of his stomach.

"The docklands?" He asked the group nervously as cold realisation washed over him. He knew exactly where Cuthbert meant. It was all anyone was talking about, these days. "There are lots of other places we can go, with music, with girls. Let's go there?"

Freddie sent him a smile. "Relax, Seth. This dock-yard darling that Cuthbert keeps wittering on about is probably terrible. We'll have one drink and then get him home, okay, old chap?"

"If only one drink would be enough," he muttered, his head lolling against the backrest. He just hoped that none of his father's spies were in The Jolly Jack at this time of night.

～

Ella

SHE KNEW the moment he'd stepped into the pub. Her skin prickled with awareness, and their eyes connected through the lively crowd that tapped their feet and clapped their hands to the music. A makeshift space for dancing had been cleared in front of her little stage tonight. Usually, knowing that she'd inspired people to dance made her wildly happy.

Ella closed her eyes and played on, her fingers

deftly moving across the strings as she tried to lose herself in the music once more. But she could see his handsome face, his eyes wary as they seemed to devour her up.

The music finished with rousing applause, and the cheers were deafening. Ella made a show of taking a bow, giving a nod to young Archie at the piano, her signal that she needed a break. Without hesitation, his fingers satisfied the crowd's desire for more music. Ella was thankful and took her time setting her fiddle back in its case, her heart thundering as she used the time to compose herself.

She had an answer to one of the many pressing questions that had plagued her recently – Seth was alive, at least. The group he'd come in with had taken a bench towards the back of the room.

She ignored them and headed for the bar, smiling, and nodding at the people who pressed in on her, who all wanted to get a little time with her. The air was smoky and heated. She needed cool and clear, but daren't risk leaving the bar in case Clara's man had decided that tonight was the night he was going to call by. She was safer inside.

"Have you seen who's crawled out of the wood-work?" Elsie murmured in her ear, directing Ella's attention to the far corner.

She didn't need to look. He sat with three other men, all as smartly dressed as he was. They'd already garnered some attention from the working girls; one was sitting on the lap of the blondest one. Judging by his rosy face, he was already three sheets to the wind drunk. Another was singing along with the ditty that Archie played.

Ella bobbed her head. The bar was obscured by people trying to get a drink, so she began to take some orders. Elsie added jugs of ale to a tray, and lifted it above her head, making her way into the throng.

"Take this!" Maud yelled into Ella's ear and tapped another tray on the bar. She pointed at the table where Seth was sitting. She opened her mouth, but her aunt was already speaking with another drinker.

Reminding herself that she was here to work, she hefted the tray and stepped into the crowd.

"Ella! Come and sit on my knee!"

"Ella, my darlin', ain't you a sight for sore eyes!"

The voices drifted through the din though she was vaguely aware of them. Her heart hammered in her chest. With practised ease, she weaved in and out of the tables, dodging the seeking, clasping hands that snaked out. When her gaze clashed with his dark and watchful stare, she banged her hip painfully on a table on a misstep. Her breath hissed out painfully, but she set the tray down without spilling a drop.

"Four ales!" She lifted them off, her words tripping over themselves as she studiously ignored the eyes boring into her profile. "Some of London's finest, too."

"Thank you, Ella." His voice made her spine stiffen but she couldn't bring herself to look at him.

It was the drunken rowdy one that grabbed her wrist. "The fiddle player! Come, join us, miss."

She surreptitiously tugged at him, her cheeks flushing. She couldn't look at Seth, couldn't bring herself to see him with his peers. They were all well-heeled, and dressed smartly, just as her father and his guests used to. These people were the ones whom he'd chosen to be with instead of her. "It's busy, sir. I am working."

"'*Sir*'!" Cuthbert cackled. "A barmaid with manners, no less!"

"Must I use my tray on that dainty head of yours?" she ground out, drawing another hearty laugh from the young man.

Undaunted, Cuthbert pulled on her arm, and she nearly lost her balance. "A girl who is as pretty as you needs a handsome man to chaperone her. Come join us, we'll take care of you. You get to pick one. Look at all these fine specimens here for you to choose from!"

"Let her go, Cuthbert," Seth's voice was quietly lethal. She did risk a look at him then and caught the danger glinting there. "Now!"

"Oh, but you can't have that one," Cuthbert cupped his free hand and added in a stage whisper as his head bob indicated Seth, "That one is engaged to be married."

Her jaw dropped as their gazes locked. She didn't even have to ask for his truth; in her heart, she already knew the answer. He belonged to another.

Feeling the pain of a thousand knives slicing into her, she yanked her arm back. Seth's companion bellowed but without a word, she whirled on her heel and pushed her way through the crowds. Fury boiled inside, humiliation burning at the back of her throat. She set the tray down, ignoring her uncle's puzzled frown when he looked at her. She needed air. She needed space. By the time she erupted through the back doors, sobs twisted in her chest.

The crescent moon illuminated the familiar yard, the stack of barrels and the line of the stone shed thrown into relief. Not a whisper of breeze was out tonight. The merriment of the public house was muted through the thick walls, yet she wallowed in the solitude. She shouldn't be out here alone, but she couldn't stay in there with him. Seth would have known that his friend's teasing had hurt her feelings and that shame burned deeper than knowing that his heart belonged to another.

Her heart pounded in her chest as she wiped her nose with the back of her hand. She stood in the shadowy enclosure, hands fisted on her hips and gulped at the cooling night air as her tears slipped down her cheeks.

She'd hoped. She'd held that little kernel of possibility to herself, that he would come back to her. She'd wanted to believe that what Seth had felt for her was enough. But he never was going to. She didn't even know why he'd come here tonight, if not to see her.

She dragged her hands down her face. He was promised to another. The woman would be beautiful and wealthy and worthy enough to meet his family's standard, that much she knew.

Stars twinkled in their inky bed as she cast her eyes to the heavens. How she longed for the comfort of her father, to seek his counsel and sage advice. She heard the footstep just a moment before the hand clamped on her shoulder and spun her around.

CHAPTER 31

Swallowing the scream trapped in her throat, it was Seth's familiar face that filled her panicked vision, instead of Clara's man.

A rush of longing hit her, and she stumbled back, out of his grip. She pressed trembling fingers to her lips to keep her cries trapped inside.

"Ella…" His voice was rough, rasping.

"How long have you been engaged, Seth?"

He stared at her impotently. "It isn't like that. I never asked her. Ironically, the only one in there who's proposed to a woman is Cuthbert, the drunken idiot, who spoke with you."

"I don't understand. He lied?"

For a moment, optimism unfurled in her chest, but his helpless shrug dashed it like a ship against the rocks. "My father and her father have struck a deal."

She balled her fists against the sudden tightness in her chest. Disbelief, hurt, anger… she stared at him, wondering if she'd ever really known him at all or if it was all simply a game to him.

A girl in every port. Isn't that what Maud had warned her about?

"Milford Shipping is in danger of collapsing, Ella. I don't have a choice."

Ella recalled a night that seemed a lifetime ago. Where she'd been manoeuvred by Clara and had Marcus Bowyer breathing down her neck. Without Cook's help, she would be Mrs Bowyer by now, no doubt imprisoned in a loveless marriage. She may even be carrying Bowyer's child by now. She could empathise with the agony that she saw in his eyes.

He continued, "My father could lose everything; the houses, the ships... It's up to me to save the company, for the sake of my mother, my brother...

Ophelia has an income that would be used to save the stricken company. Her father owns warehouses in America that we need to store and move goods over there. He has links to the railways out there, too. The Harrisons have the money that could save the company."

She studied him in the eerie light. "I thought you were different but you're just like her."

"Who?"

"My stepmother, Clara," she spat. "You'd both sell your soul for money."

"Ella–"

She dodged away from the hand he'd held out. "Your family look down on people like me. We're worthless because we have nothing and yet here, amongst the folks that your father holds such disdain for, I've seen people with nothing give away their last slice of bread to feed a starving child.

I've been in your world, Seth. I grew up privileged. I had a nice house. My father made bad business decisions and we lost everything. But I'd much rather be here – right here and now – in this docklands pub. Because I know who my enemies are. Here, in the lowest that society has, I've known loyalty like never before."

"Please, I can't stand to see you like this."

"Then go," she told him thickly. "Just turn around and walk away. Go back to your world. Leave me to mine."

Seth stared at her; the sharp planes of his face etched in misery. "Would it help if I said I did it for you?"

"I don't believe you," she said. "I'll never believe you again."

"It's true," Seth ground out, taking a step towards her. "My father found out about us. He threatened you, Ella. I couldn't risk it–"

She rounded on him, eyes blazing. "Tell him to join the queue! I already have my stepmother and some unknown stranger looking for me. Your father is just an extra in a list of many people wanting to make me disappear!"

Even in the low light, she could see the confusion

reflected on his face. "What do you mean? What stranger? Are you in danger?"

She wrapped her arms around her middle. "Go back to your world, Seth. I can sleep easy at night knowing that you're alive, at least."

"Ella, if you're in danger–"

"She isn't," James' voice was quietly spoken. Ella hadn't even noticed her uncle had walked out of the back of The Jolly Jack. He held the back door of the pub open, watching them both. "She has friends here, Milford.

There's a carriage out the front. Your friends are in it, waiting for you. The drunk one is furious that he's been thrown out of a dockyard public house. I wouldn't keep him waiting if I were you. He's slinging insults at sailors, and that's never a good idea."

Seth dithered, as if torn between his two worlds. "Ella, please."

"Leave her be, son. You've stated your case. I don't envy you having to marry out of duty. I hope that she's a good woman," James let go of the door and stepped further into the yard. Ella felt bolstered when he stood next to her, a fatherly hand about her shoulders. "Married life can be arduous with the wrong person."

The ball of pain in her stomach clenched when Seth continued to look at her. His eyes traversed her face as if committing it to memory before he turned and ducked through the back door to The Jolly Jack.

The door swung shut, the sounds of the swarm inside rising and falling. She blinked, the action causing her tears to spill down her cheeks. Her mouth wobbled from the effort of holding in her sobs as realisation crashed in on her.

James squeezed her shoulder gently. "You did the right thing, my girl."

My girl. Just like her father used to call her. She nodded, her heart heavy with unrequited love. "Why does it hurt so?"

James turned her into his chest, patting her back gently. The gesture, so much like how Henry would turn her to him, caused the fragile hold she had on her emotions to break. She sobbed into his shirt, crying for all that she had lost.

THE RAIN HAD BEEN UNRELENTING for days, the downpour making the London streets slick with puddles and mud.

Ships came and went, rolling in the choppy waters as the sailors and the dockworkers braved the elements day in and day out. Mists clung to the buildings, hiding the masts of the boats so that everything was otherworldly.

At night, she served ale and whisky, knowing that her aunt and uncle were watching her out of concern. She tried her best to fill her time and lift her spirits but not even her music was enough to ease the pain in her heart.

The streets were bustling. A frenetic energy that not

even the miserable weather could staunch. Barrels rumbled along the cobbles. Drays squeaked past. People called out their cheery greetings to her as she wound her way back towards the harbour.

She knew that she could take one of the many alleys from the market back to The Jolly Jack. She would probably find a little bit of shelter along the narrowed walkways between the tall buildings. But, like picking a scab, she chose to walk along the main thoroughfare, and past Milford's shipping offices. Even as she told herself to keep her eyes on the cobblestones, she couldn't help but glance up at the window, hoping to catch a glimpse of him.

But the office was dark and empty, with no sign of life. Her heart sank even further. He wasn't there. Since the confrontation in the yard, she'd only seen fleeting glimpses of people that she assumed were clerks.

She pulled her shawl tighter around her shoulders, trying to ward off the chill that was settling into her bones. She trudged through the puddles, uncaring that the hem of her dress was getting soaked with each step.

She had told him to leave her alone, but she missed him terribly. In the week since they had spoken, she wondered if she'd made a horrible mistake. Was it stubbornness or pride that had cost her the one person who'd cared for her? As that thought slid into her mind, she cursed herself for being a lovesick fool. He'd led her a merry dance, hadn't he? Slumming it with a docklands barmaid when his heart held affection for the upmarket Ophelia.

She rounded the street corner, head bent against the steady torrent. Lost in her thoughts, she put her shoulder into the front door of the pub.

"It's raining cats and dogs out there!" She huffed, setting her basket down.

"Ella?"

She was busy peeling her shawl off and looked up. "Hmm?"

James was standing at the bar, though it wasn't his careful expression that drew her gaze. Her mouth dropped open, her stuttering mind struggling to catch up with what she was seeing. She took a tentative step forward as she stared at the slight figure standing next to the bar.

"Milly? What on earth are you doing here?"

"It's Thomas, miss. He needs you."

CHAPTER 32

"*T*homas?" Ella croaked. The simple question sent dread racing along her spine. "What's wrong with him?"

Milly's sombre expression didn't lift. "I'm afraid it's quite a mess, Miss. And Thomas needs your help."

"Where is his mother?"

"If I may," James interrupted. "Why don't you both take a seat near the fire? I'll get Maud to make you each some tea. I could do with a whisky myself."

Milly stared at her Uncle James. Perhaps she saw the uncanny resemblance to Henry, too. She gave him a slight nod as Ella showed her to the fire. The public house was empty but there were still the smells of sweet ale and smoke filling the space.

The maid was just as sodden as she was, her thin coat having done nothing against the elements.

"I can't quite believe my eyes," Ella said as she took a

seat next to the fire. The heat did little to dissipate the shivers that convulsed their bodies.

"I thought I would never see you again," Milly echoed her own thoughts.

"Did you travel it all this way by yourself?"

"That I did, Miss," Milly said. She leaned back as James set two steaming cups of tea on the table in front of them. Without asking, he pulled out a chair and settled into one of the chairs. "The door of the pub is locked, so we have a little while to talk."

"Milly is a dear friend of mine," Ella told her uncle, reaching for the cup. She wrapped her hands gratefully around the heat but didn't take a sip as she stared at her friend. "She was in Father's employ."

The flames of the fire danced in his blue eyes as he looked at the young maid and back, "She said as much when she hammered on the door until I opened it. After our recent visitor, I was a little reluctant to believe her."

Ella saw the frown on Milly's face though she didn't want her to know that Clara had sent people after her. "If I'm being truthful, I owe Milly my life."

James lifted his glass of whiskey in a toast. "Then you are a welcome guest in my home, dear girl."

A smile ghosted over Milly's face. "Thank you, sir. You look like your brother."

James' lips hooked up on one side. "So, I'm told but we can catch up later. Please, what's this about Thomas needing help."

"It's a long story, you see. Things haven't been good,

miss. At first, when you left, they were easier. The marriage happened. Thomas was sent to the school, just as was planned but then your stepmother found out about the other woman."

"What other woman?" Ella asked.

"It seems there was a long-term mistress here in the city. The arguments... well, they grew ferocious. Sharp-tongued and vicious. The master," Milly caught herself, and eyed Ella carefully. "That is, the Doctor, he was spending time here in the city, and your step-mother was home alone."

"That couldn't have been nice for you all."

"You know how she gets on," Milly muttered. "Cook left. Your stepmother knew one of us had had a hand in your leaving. She knew it couldn't have been me. She was just awful, miss." She was staring into her tea.

Culpability over having left them all to deal with the aftermath of her escape weighed in on her. "I'm sorry that you had to go through that, Milly."

She raised her eyes. "The doctor... he's dead, miss."

Ella exchanged a look with James, apprehension prickling her skin. "Dead?"

Milly nodded.

"H-how did he die?"

"It was terrible, miss," Milly whispered, her voice raw. Ella leaned over to pat the girl's hand. "Just like..."

Ella didn't have to try hard to imagine. She remembered the agony her father had been in. Her eyes grew hot. Frowning, she blinked, trying to get her emotions in check. "Had he been ill?"

"He'd been sickening for a while, taking his Fowler's solution."

Ella recognised it. Her father had had the same one. It eased his digestive problems and had invigorated him, though Ella had long since wondered what was in them because they'd not made her father better at all.

"He refused to take it from... from Mrs Seward, you know, after your father."

James sat up, a brow hooking up. "Seward? Her married name is Seward?"

"Y-yes, sir," Milly said.

"It's in the papers, Ella," The glass hit the table and James leaned forward in earnest. "Haven't you seen them?"

Ella hadn't heard a thing. She'd been so consumed with Seth, with everything that had happened, she'd not taken notice of anything else. She shook her head.

"A young wife has been arrested for the murder of a well-known doctor..." James' voice trailed off. "*That's* Clara?"

Milly nodded; her expression grim. "It is indeed. That's why I'm here. Thomas is bereft. He had no one, now that... that the doctor has gone. Mrs Seward is protesting her innocence, of course."

"I don't understand," Ella muttered, rubbing at the ache that had suddenly gathered in her temples. "Why has Clara been arrested?"

"Because the doctor Seward's colleagues claim that he was poisoned, miss."

CHAPTER 33

*E*lla stood in the grand lobby of the hotel, feeling small and out of place among the elegantly dressed women and men bustling about. The marble floors gleamed beneath her worn boots, with grey daylight pouring from the domed roof that soared over her head.

Her shabby dark dress made her stand out in stark contrast to the luxurious surroundings, and she was acutely aware of the strange looks that she was getting from the wealthy, fashionable guests who hurried by her.

She willed Milly to hurry up, feeling distinctly uncomfortable. Perhaps she'd be less conspicuous at the edges of the room. She began to tug at the hem of her dress, making her way across the fancy floor until she collided with someone, causing her to stumble.

"Pardon me, I...," A pair of hands held her by the elbow, though the voice trailed off when she looked up to see Seth. Their eyes met, and for a moment, Ella was frozen in place.

She watched his shock slide to pleasure on his face, though that soon edged into something sad. His eyes searched her face before he spoke. "Ella," he said, his voice low and hesitant. "I'm sorry, I didn't see you there."

He looked dashingly smart in his top hat and suit. The joy that bloomed in her stuttering heart was over-shadowed by pain when the clouds moved into his eyes, and she saw the shutters come down on his face. He let her go, his hands flexing at his sides.

Her hands moved to rub at the spots where his fingers had tightened on her arms. "What are you doing here?"

"I could ask you the same question," he said, his gaze moving about the crowds that surged around them. "You're a long way from Wapping."

Ella's spine stiffened with indignation. "Am I too low-born for such an establishment?"

Irritation flickered in his expression. "That was a cheap shot, Ella."

Before she could apologise, Milly called her name. Ella turned and looked across the lobby. The girl beck-oned to her. Ella's eyes moved past the well-heeled unfamiliar young man standing next to Milly and lit upon Thomas. He was fidgeting, his gaze meeting Ella's and then quickly sliding away as he adjusted his neck collar. He looked lost and broken. Even from this distance, she could see the anguish on his face.

James was right. It didn't matter that they didn't share blood. She had been raised with him as her brother. Right now, he needed her.

"I have to go," she murmured distractedly at Seth and hurried towards Thomas.

Her brother's face collapsed into tears as she neared him. She was vaguely aware of Milly introducing the man next to her as Mr Grimley, a teacher from Thomas' school who'd escorted him down from the campus. Ella nodded her greeting and allowed Mr Grimley to steer the group through the door behind them. She followed the group down the corridor and into a small lounge. Her focus was on her brother.

She didn't know how she was going to help him with this mess that Clara had created, only that she had to.

SETH WATCHED her hurry away from him without a backward glance, frowning at her retreating back.

He watched the exchange between the group with avid curiosity. The young woman was dressed like a servant and Ella greeted her warmly enough, but it was the well-heeled man that ushered her through the door that speared jealousy through him. Seth didn't miss the admiring glance he was giving her.

"Seth!" His mother's voice rang across the crowd.

Reluctantly, he pulled his gaze from the closing

door. His mother waved him over to where his sister was standing. "Hello, Mother. Prudence."

"Why were you standing in the middle of the floor like that?" His sister asked, tugging at the fingertips of her gloves. "What were you looking at?"

"Where have you been?" He asked, frustration sharpening his voice. He dutifully leaned down and bussed his cheek to his mother's, then his sister's, even as his mind raced ahead. Who were those people that Ella was with? Was she in danger? He should go and check, although she had greeted the girl and the youngest boy with an embrace. "Your letter said lunch at one o'clock sharp. I thought that I was late and came rushing in here."

"What can I say?" His sister shrugged in only the way an indulged younger child could. "London traffic is abominable. Anyway, why are you in such a foul mood?"

"I'm not," Seth muttered, his gaze sliding surreptitiously to the closed door. Perhaps he should run across there. Did she need rescuing? What would his mother say about him ruining her luncheon plans?

"We're sorry we're late, dear," His mother patted his arm. "But we're here now. Let's not start with a quarrel. I want to have lunch with my children and have a nice time doing it."

Seth had almost turned down the invitation, but he couldn't think of a valid reason to say no. Sarah flagged down a porter. "Can you let Mr Paskell know that we're here?"

"Your name?"

"Milford," Sarah said as if the porter should have known this information. "I swear, this place is getting more common by the day," she added in a mutter as the porter made a beeline for the lounge.

Seth didn't bother to disguise his disgust. So much for thinking he should find Ella and introduce her to his family.

"What was that look for?"

"Never mind," Seth shook his head at his mother as they were escorted into the salon.

Scents of food filled the room. Matching bone china and shining cutlery adorned the white linen tables. In the corner, a small group played a pleasant symphony. His appetite vanished even as he took his seat. He couldn't see through the wide doors into the lobby from this angle. He tried to concentrate on what his mother and sister were saying. The words that the waiter was telling them danced through his mind without registering. Only one thought held fast: just what was going on across the lobby?

CHAPTER 34

*M*illy held the door open for Ella and she waited until it fully shut before speaking. "Do you think Thomas will be okay, miss?"

Ella waited for her friend to fall into step next to her. "He has a sensible head on his shoulders. I'm sure that once the dust has settled, then he will be fine."

Her brother had grown up a little, but upon seeing her, he had promptly burst into tears. Fortunately, his time at school had shielded him from the worst of recent events. Ella knew all too well the spitefulness and the torrid arguments that Milly spoke of, although she was certain that the fallout of his mother's arrest would haunt Thomas forever.

From Milly and Thomas's stories, Ella pieced together that the Seward's marriage had swiftly crumbled once Clara uncovered her husband's mistress. A woman who'd been in his life for much longer than Clara.

Bitter disputes had ensued, both behind closed doors and in public. Dr Seward, although older than Henry, was otherwise hale and hearty. His sudden death raised suspicions among his colleagues when they discovered a significant amount of 'nux vomica' missing from his cabinet.

Clara, in tears and hysterics, had been questioned by the police. The new cook confirmed that Clara had uncharacteristically baked treats for her husband on the day of his demise – a rarity since Henry Tomlinson's passing.

Ella discreetly inquired about the mysterious substance with Mr Grimley, who revealed it to be an opiate—strychnine—commonly used as a lethal poison for pest control. Ingesting it led to excruciating muscle spasms, foaming at the mouth, and ultimately asphyxiation. All too clearly, the memory of her father writhing in agony resurfaced, and despite her disdain for Dr Seward's actions after Henry's death, she couldn't help but pity him. Clara, it seemed, had assumed she could get away with murder again, but this time, she lacked the protection of a respected doctor to hide her crimes.

Ella had almost blurted out that her father had died in similar circumstances, but she hadn't wanted to add to Thomas' burden. Besides, she only had her memories. Would that be enough for the police, or would she be viewed as a scorned young woman who'd been cast out of her childhood home?

Milly walked beside her down the richly carpeted

hallway. "But without official acknowledgement of his parentage, what will happen to Dr Seward's fortune?"

Ella was dismayed to discover that Clara had told Thomas of his true paternity – the much wealthier prospect of Albert Seward. It seemed that even the school had been apprised of this fact, too, from Thomas. Ella silently fumed over Clara's callousness towards both Henry and Thomas, which was compounded when Mr Grimley assured her that, without irrefutable proof of his bloodline, Thomas would probably have no more claim on the Seward fortune than she would.

"I don't know, Milly. I shall speak with my uncle, and hope that he may know of someone who can advise Thomas better."

"Do you think it worth a visit to Clara?"

Ella stopped to stare at the maid. Just the thought filled her with revulsion. "To what end? You heard Mr Grimley. Clara is telling anyone who'd listen that she'd the victim of a cover-up by the doctor's colleagues."

"Miss Tomlinson?"

Ella looked back toward the lounge that they'd been using, and Mr Grimley gave them a little wave. She schooled her face into her polite smile. The teacher might be young, but he'd been a steadying voice in the room as she'd spoken to Thomas.

"I'm glad I caught you," he said, checking the door to the lounge was still closed. "I wanted to speak with you in private."

252

Milly backed away but Ella stopped her, needing the silent support of her friend. "Is Thomas okay?"

"He's fine. I dare say much better since seeing his sister," he added kindly.

Her smile warmed up a notch. "Well, despite Thomas' lineage, my father had a hand in raising him. He was a decent and honest man."

"As I said earlier, the school are quite happy for Thomas to stay on. His fees are paid up to the end of the year. I know that some of the founding members are a tad worried about the school possibly being involved in a scandal that is splashed across the newspapers…"

"I'm afraid there isn't much I can do about that, Mr Grimley," Ella replied.

"I know. Thomas has mentioned that his mother wishes for him to visit her."

"I don't think that would be good for him," Ella said. "Even if Thomas is agreeable, his mother can be quite persuasive, and dastardly with it. I will speak with my uncle. Perhaps Thomas can stay with him during the holidays, or at least until the house and the doctor's estate are resolved."

Ella saw from his expression that she wasn't saying anything that hadn't occurred to him. "Dr Seward was a very generous benefactor to the school. His family have a long association with us. We have legal representatives who send their sons to us. I wondered about asking the headmaster to act on your behalf?"

"That would be very helpful," Ella said.

"I will escort him back to the school but…" Mr Grimley turned his attention to Milly. "I was wondering, if it's not too much trouble, perhaps you could stay with Thomas. He seems to like having someone familiar near him."

Milly's brows met as she looked at Ella, seeking permission.

"It's up to you, Milly," Ella reassured her friend. "You are in no way obligated. You have done more than enough by seeking me out, and remaining behind to ensure that the house is packed away safely."

Milly swallowed, her cheeks reddening under such praise. "It's not like I had much else to do, miss. My employer being a murderess and that," her mouth twitched on one side, which teased a smile out of Ella.

"Thank goodness for you, Milly," Ella breathed, gripping her friend's hand. "I have missed you."

"Will you stay on? For Thomas?" Mr Grimley prompted them when they were smiling at each other.

Milly swung her gaze back to him. "Yes."

"Do you need money for a cab, Milly?" Ella asked.

"I shall take good care of her," Mr Grimley stopped her when she began to search in her pockets for some coins. "I'll make sure she is returned to wherever she needs to go."

"Very well," Ella murmured once Milly had given her an encouraging nod. "I'd best hurry. My uncle is waiting for me down the street."

She bade them each goodbye with a promise to stay in touch. They each were tasked with finding ways to help her brother whilst his life imploded. She straight-armed her way through the door at the end of the corridor and erupted back into the main lobby.

Her mind was so preoccupied with thoughts of the morning's developments that she hadn't heard her name being called until Seth pulled her around to face him. She'd almost forgotten about him.

"Seth. I thought you…" She looked at the row of seats against the wall where he'd been sitting. "What are you still doing here?"

His gaze raked over her distressed face. "I was worried about you. Who were those people I saw you with?"

Thoughts tumbled over each other like a kaleido-scope, including all her troubles since Milly had shown up out of the blue yesterday which almost eclipsed her heartache over Seth. She could tell him that it was none not his concern, but she didn't have it in her to be cruel to him, today of all days. But to unburden her truth here and now would not be wise.

"That is a very long story for another day." She dug her thumbs into her gritty eyes. When her hands fell away, he was staring intently at her. It would be so easy to step into his arms, to take solace in them, even for just a moment, but she couldn't do that to herself. "I don't wish to be rude, but I have much to do, Seth."

It was Seth's double-take that drew her attention to the two people behind him when his name was called out, the voice snappy and loud. Ella didn't need an introduction to either of the women who were walking toward them.

Their clothing was stylish, in similar shades of blue. Their jewellery was opulent and sparkled in the light from the overhead chandeliers. The older woman had the same dark colouring and perceptive eyes as her son. The younger woman, following behind her, had a much lighter colouring. Ella could tell that they were mother and daughter.

"I'm sorry," Seth muttered to Ella under his breath. "I thought they'd be in the salon much longer."

"Seth?" The woman's shrill voice carried across the space between them. Her eyes didn't waiver once from Ella, taking in her faded dress, and tatty boots. Ella caught the censorship in her look and gritted her teeth. "Have you concluded your business already? Where is Charles?" Mrs Milford's gaze flitted to her son before settling once more on Ella.

"No, I...I never left."

His mother's frown was formidable as she turned the full force of her glare onto her son. "You said you had to rush off to meet your clerk. Is *she* why you were distracted all during luncheon?"

Seth's temper matched his mother's. "If you must know, then yes. Mother, this is my friend, Miss Ella Tomlinson. Ella, I'd like to introduce you to my mother, Mrs Sarah Milford, and my sister, Mrs Prudence Donovan."

Ella bobbed a curtsy to the woman, whose nostrils had now turned white. Prudence seemed positively gleeful at her brother's obvious discomfort which made Ella wonder about the dynamics of the family that had nurtured Seth. "Very pleased to make your acquaintance."

"I can't say the feeling is mutual," Sarah muttered, her lips barely moving. "How do you know my son?"

Ella considered lying to them, but Seth beat her to it. "Ella's uncle owns a business down at the docklands."

Sarah Milford's surprise was evident as she studied Ella. "You're in shipping, too?"

"No, Mother," Seth explained impatiently. "He owns a public house. I eat there regularly. Ella is a talented musician."

"Wait," Prudence interrupted, staring at Ella with renewed interest. "You're the Dockyard Darling, aren't you?"

"The *what*?" Sarah asked her daughter.

Ella's patience with them ran out. Sarah Milford's demeanour had elements of Clara's cruelty in her, and she had no desire to tangle with such a woman. She'd asked her uncle to give her an hour after he'd insisted that he accompany her into the city. She'd argued that she had nothing to worry about now that Clara was incapacitated but James was insistent.

She wasn't sure how long it had been since she'd left him down the street, but she didn't want him to come barrelling in here looking for her.

"Yes, I am," she said to Prudence. "I'm very sorry but I must go. My uncle is waiting for me. It was very nice meeting you both." Without waiting for a response, she hitched up her skirts and turned, hurrying through the brass and wooden doors. She'd reached the bottom of the steps before Seth caught her up.

"Ella, wait!"

Impatience zipped through her. "I don't have the time for this, Seth. My uncle is waiting for me and–"

Seth interrupted her, his eyes flashing. "I gave you an introduction to my family and you run away? I thought that was what you wanted?"

Ella glanced back at the hotel. The rain had stopped but windows reflected the grey and dismal skies. She imagined his mother to be watching them through the glass. "Now is not the time nor the place for this, Seth." She shook her head at him and retreated further down the street.

In two long strides, he'd caught her again, uncaring of the attention that he was drawing from the patrons and passers-by. "Ella, why are you here at this hotel? Who was that man? Is he your lover?"

"You have no place asking me those types of questions," she snapped. "Not when you're engaged to be married to another!"

He gripped her then, hauling her up by her arms, his eyes blazing. "Stop shutting me out! Every time we get close to talking about you, you change the subject."

She was filled with indignation as she struggled against the restraints of his touch. She jutted her chin out, challenge raging in her gaze, "Because the truth would confirm every bad thing that your father fears over you getting involved with someone like me!" His angry face blurred through her tears and the biting grip he had on her arms lessened. "My father was murdered, Seth," she admitted miserably.

Slowly, he lowered her back to the ground. Doubt clouded is his dark look. "What?"

"It's true," she told him dully, "though I have no proof. The two men that you saw me speaking with? The older of the two is a teacher, escorting the younger one, who is my brother, Thomas – except, he isn't my blood." She swiped uselessly at the tears that ran down her cheeks. "Clara cheated on my father. Thomas isn't my father's child. I found out her secret and she threatened to have me committed to an asylum if I ever breathed a word. I fled in the night, helped by the cook. The young girl I was with was a maid in my father's employ – she's also my dearest friend who stepped up to help my brother when she didn't have to.

I didn't want to tell you any of this because I barely understand it myself. All I know is that your father is right – you are best not to involve yourself in this situation. Becoming entangled in this whole mess will do untold damage to your business because my stepmother is currently in prison after being accused of killing her second husband – Thomas' father. Both men died in very similar circumstances. I cannot be responsible for dragging you down." He relinquished his hold on her and she took a step back. Her heart ached and she offered him a watery smile. "I do love you, Seth Milford, but you must forget about me. My brother needs me now. I… I wish you all the very best happiness for you and your fiancée."

This time when she darted across the street Seth didn't follow her. She weaved in and out of the pedestrians, the carts and the street rats, to where James waited for her. She had so much to do. She hoped that her uncle would have some answers for her. She would return to the docklands, back to where she felt safe, and try to work out what her future would be now.

Seth watched her go.

Her story sounded so fantastical that he knew it must be true. She was a proud woman. To confess the way that she did would have cost her dearly and yet, his heart felt lighter than it had in the longest of times.

He waited until she'd blended into the sea of people that filled the busy street before he walked back into the hotel. He found his mother just where he knew she'd be – at the window, watching their exchange. Not knowing what was said would be driving her mad.

"Who was that woman, Seth?"

"And why were you manhandling her in the street?" Prudence added as she leaned over her mother's shoulder.

A faint smile tinged his lips. His family were nothing if not predictable. "What did you think of her?"

"What did I–" Sarah stared at her son in horror. "A

dockland musician in rags? Is she wealthy? Does she come from a good family?"

"She isn't wealthy, no. I've only met her uncle."

"Seth, what are you doing with your life? You're meant to be engaged to Ophelia."

"Well, I liked her," Prudence replied to her brother's original question. "She has spunk."

Sarah shook her head in exasperation, glaring at her two smirking children. "My mother warned me that families would test me to the nth degree, and I fear that she has finally been proved correct."

"Oh, Mama," Prudence said. "Seth was never going to marry that frightful bore."

Sarah gaped at her daughter. She took a surreptitious look about and lowered her voice. "We'll discuss this later. After I've had a lie-down."

"No time," Seth dropped a kiss on his mother's cheek. "I really do have to meet Charles. Will Father be at Linton Manor later?"

"Yes, why?"

"Good. How about I come up for the evening?"

Usually, his mother had to pester him for a visit to the country. She narrowed her eyes suspiciously. "What for?"

"I want to tell him that I've fallen deeply in love with a fiddle player," he pecked his sister on the cheek. "Prudence, I think Mother might need some smelling salts. I will see you both later. Safe travels."

CHAPTER 35

 eth

SETH WAITED, watching as the seconds ticked by. The longer he waited, the angrier his father became. Finally, Philip Milford exploded, his face turning a deep shade of red.

"Out of the question!" he roared, slamming his fist down on the table. Plates and cutlery went flying, and Sarah let out a cry as she tried to save her wine goblet from spilling. "No son of mine will be allowed to walk away from this business. I have sweated and bled for you, my son, as did my father and his father before that."

Seth remained calm, though his heart was racing. He knew that this conversation would not be an easy one, but he had to stay true to his convictions. "I'm well aware of all that you and Grandfather have done for us," he said, his voice steady. "But it can't be denied that your recent business decisions have had dire consequences. I warned you that purchasing such a colossal boat was not in our best interests, and now the effects of that poor decision have come to fruition."

Philip Milford surged to his feet; his face contorted with rage. "Who do you think you are?"

Seth stood too, meeting his father's gaze. "My decision is final, Father. I am not going to marry Ophelia Harrison, and I am relinquishing any financial ownership of Milford Shipping."

He turned to his mother, his expression softening when he saw her eyes glistening with tears. "I'm sorry, Mother," he said, as gently as he could. "I know that you had high hopes for a grand society wedding, but the truth is that I just don't love the girl. I never could."

He nodded to each of them and walked away from the dining table. As he reached for the door handle, his mother's voice stopped him in his tracks. "It's that girl, isn't it?" she asked. "The one you were speaking to in the hotel earlier today."

"What girl?" Philip demanded, his tone scathing.

Seth squared his shoulders, determined to speak his truth. "If you must know, then yes," he said firmly. "She is a wonderfully talented musician, but her family is not a wealthy one."

"You're throwing away your future for a bit of skirt?" Philip sneered.

Seth felt his temper beginning to boil. "Careful,

Father," he said, his voice low. "I intend to marry that 'bit of skirt', and she will be your daughter-in-law, whether you choose to acknowledge it or not."

"I warned you what would happen to her if you continued your ridiculous dalliance!"

"Philip!" Sarah gasped. "You knew of this?"

"Of course," Philip snapped. "There isn't anything this pillock does without my knowledge."

"You will leave her alone," Seth jabbed a finger toward the ground to punctuate his words. "I mean it, Father. You leave both of us alone."

"Then you are as good as dead to me, my boy," Philip said, his voice cold. "Get out of my house and never darken my doorstep again."

Seth felt a pang of sadness as he heard his father's words, even as Sarah begged Philip to take them back. Seth knew that he had made the right decision. He executed a mocking half-bow and quickly left the room, his mind already racing with plans for his future.

Dwyer was hovering in the hallway, no doubt eavesdropping. Seth requested his carriage be brought to the front of the house and hurried up to his child-hood room, packing his belongings with care. As he looked around the familiar space for what he knew would be the last time, he felt a mixture of sadness and excitement. He was leaving behind everything that he had ever known, but he was also stepping boldly into his future.

Seth jogged down the wide staircase, coming to a halt when he rounded the turn and he saw his parents loitering in the hallway. He let out a heartfelt sigh as he slowly descended the remaining stairs.

"Please," he said tiredly. "I've had enough fighting for tonight. I know that I've hurt you both, but I don't want to quarrel anymore."

He moved to walk around his parents, but Sarah spoke up, "Tell him, Philip."

Seth looked at them both, his face a mask of confusion. "Tell me what?"

His father's mouth flattened into a mutinous line as he stared off into the distance.

Sarah growled in frustration. "You're as stubborn as that mule in the field down the road," she told her husband. "The company is in–"

"There isn't much of a bloody company left," Philip snapped.

"What are you talking about, Father?"

"You were right," Philip declared, throwing his hands apart with a bark of disbelief. "Does that make you happy? I should never have bought that boat. It's more than set us back, it's ruined us."

Seth looked at his father sharply. "I know that we have had problems, but it can't be as bad as all that. I've seen the books. We have a lot of shipments due to us."

"The market is so flooded with some products, it's driven the price of even our most profitable lines into the ground," Philip said wearily. "We're not just floundering, we're in dire straits."

Seth blinked, lowering his case to the floor. His

father was weary and for the first time in Seth's memory, he looked aged. "What are you going to do?"

"I need you, Seth." Philip Milford had dedicated his life to this business. Seth could see the toll it had taken etched into his father's face. "I know that you have other obligations, but I need you. Help me, son. Save the company."

Seth's resolve wavered. Ella had told him that she loved him, and he knew that he loved her in return. As soon as she'd said those words to him, he'd known that he wanted to hear them every day for the rest of his life. But duty was a deeply rooted obligation in his life. He couldn't simply abandon his family's legacy now.

"I cannot marry Ophelia Harrison just for money," he said, his hands going to his hips. "I'd be no better than a girl lifting her skirts at the docks – sorry, mother," he added when Sarah caught the shocked gasp behind her gloved hand. "But I refuse to do it."

"In all honesty, Seth, whilst the Harrison warehouses would be useful, her money is just a drop in the ocean for what we need." Philip fixed Seth with a repentant look. "I did not mean what I said."

"I won't change my mind about Ella," Seth informed him. "But I do have an idea that might just help Milford Shipping."

Philip's face brightened. "What is it?"

Seth smiled. "Why don't you let me put my case back in my room, then I'll meet you both in the drawing room?"

"Dwyer can do that," Philip pressed the door back. "I want to hear your idea."

"Very well." Seth felt a sense of relief wash over him as he walked past his father. If he could get his father on board with his new ideas, then perhaps there was a chance for him to convince Ella that she was the one for him, after all.

CHAPTER 36

lla

"I TOLD YOU ALREADY," James said from behind the bar. "You should've brought Thomas here. Henry would've wanted me to keep the boy safe."

Ella set down the glasses on the bar top. "I know you made that kind offer, uncle, but Thomas wanted to remain in school. Besides, we don't have the funds to help him. Are you sure you don't know anybody who knows the law?"

"You know the kind that we have drinking in here," retorted Maud. "Sailors and lowborn."

Ella's expression softened as she looked at her aunt. "Good, kind, and honest folk."

"Nothing like your stepmother," Elsie added.

Beyond the windows of the Jolly Jack, the summer

rain fell. Grey clouds rolled along, the mists lingering over the Thames. They were enjoying the afternoon lull between lunchtime and when dockers came looking for their supper. Ella hadn't slept much the night before and was grateful to have work to keep her occupied.

"It's a shame Thomas's parentage is in question," Ella said. "Dr Seward was a wealthy man. His estate would be more than enough to cover Thomas's school fees and other living expenses."

"Most people would have turned their backs on the boy," Maud said to her. "After all, Thomas wasn't there for you when you needed him."

"Thomas is a young boy with an impressionable mind," Ella reminded her aunt.

"And Clara is a master manipulator," James added. "She has certainly gotten far in life."

"Coldbath Fields prison isn't all that far," Elsie chuckled.

"You could always ask your Mr Milford," Maud suggested.

"Out of the question," James retorted, his face as dour as the weather. "She doesn't need more complications, Maud. She needs people who want to be here and who want to help her."

Ella was touched that her uncle had rushed to her defence. She knew he was right, of course, but after her outburst yesterday in the street, she wasn't sure she could ever face Seth Milford again.

The door of the Jolly Jack had swelled in the rain. It

rattled before it cracked open. All four of them turned to look in unison, although Ella's heart rate settled when it was a mousey old gentleman who stepped through the door.

He removed his hat, shaking off the rain droplets as his shrewd eyes travelled the group in front of him. He had the appearance of a man who spent many hours away from sunlight, not the thug that James and Elsie had met. His thinning hair was wispy and combed over his head. He gave a tentative smile as he stepped further into the bar.

"I wonder if you can help me?" He said to Ella. "Might you be Miss Elizabeth Tomlinson?"

Ella's heart knocked against her rib cage. Only one man had used her full name. She glanced at her uncle, seeking confirmation that this was the man who had been looking for her. But her uncle's puzzled expression told her that he didn't know who he was either.

"That depends on who's asking," James said, as he swung under the bar hatch and placed himself between the stranger and Ella.

Unperturbed by the subtle threat, the mousey man gave a little chuckle and set his hat and briefcase on one of the tables. "My good man, I mean no trouble to you. But if you could be so kind as to fetch me a pint of your finest ale, and perhaps some food?"

James didn't move. He folded his arms and glowered at the arrival.

The man seemed unfazed by James' aggression, instead choosing to brush off his jacket and adjust his spectacles. "My apologies, sir. My name is George Harris, and I represent the law firm of Clancy, Burke, and Harris. I am here to speak with Miss Elizabeth Tomlinson regarding a matter of great importance."

James' arms lowered. "What matter would that be?"

Mr Harris leaned over to the side to peer around the breadth of her uncle. "You are Miss Tomlinson, yes?"

She exchanged a worried glance with Maud, her heart sinking. Reluctantly, she nodded.

Mr Harris pressed his hands together as if in supplication to the Heavens. "You have been the most troublesome girl to find. I sent my two best agents. It seems they had to hunt you the length and breadth of this beautiful country."

The cold knot of fear in her stomach tightened. "You sent people to look for me? They weren't from Clara?"

Mr Harris shuddered. "Your father's widow? Goodness, no."

"Then what do you want?" James growled at him. "You've terrorised my niece with your lackeys. Clara made all sorts of threats against her. Tried to force her to marry, trying to eradicate my brother from her life. What else were we meant to think other than it was coming from her?"

Mr Harris conveyed his disappointment, and he pressed his hands together once more. "Please, forgive me. It did not occur to me that she would have threatened you. If I caused you any worry, then I sincerely apologise."

For the first time, Ella stepped out from behind her uncle. Her hands were twisted into her skirts. "Why are you here, Mr Harris?"

Harris leaned in, his voice dropping to a low whisper. "It concerns the estate of your late father, miss. There are certain documents that require your signature, and without them, the estate cannot be settled."

Ella's mind raced as she tried to make sense of it all. "My father had no estate. He died penniless. That was why Clara had to marry again so soon."

Harris smiled, his demeanour shifting to one of warmth and friendliness. "If you would be so kind as to join me for a moment, Miss Tomlinson, I would be happy to explain everything in detail."

CHAPTER 37

eth

His mother had retired to bed shortly after she'd ensured that her firstborn and her husband weren't going to fight anymore. His father had hemmed and hawed over some of Seth's ideas, but it was pleasing to know that the two of them could see an eye-to-eye future.

He'd gone to bed but had been too excited to sleep. He'd waited for dawn, watching the pink and purple hues streaking the sky. As soon as he'd heard the scullery maid setting the fires down below him, he'd summoned the carriage to take him to the train station to meet the seven o'clock train.

Every station stop on the way towards London had

felt like an interminable wait until finally, he passed under the Euston arch and into the first waiting carriage he found. The sun was past its zenith, and he knew that the Jolly Jack would be past the lunchtime rush by the time he got through the city traffic.

He'd rehearsed what he would say to Ella but as the ship masts of the docklands came into view on the horizon up ahead, some of his courage left him. Ella was not like any woman he'd ever known before. He'd always been so assured around the fairer sex; he could predict what would come out of their mouths – but not with her. She was an independent thinker, and stubborn. What would happen if she refused him?

The carriage rolled to a stop, and he'd opened the door and got out before the driver had had time to turn in his seat. Seth flipped him an extra coin as he'd hopped down into the street, which earned him a hearty hat tip and a quick grin.

He hurried along the damp cobbled streets, his heart pounding with the weight of the declaration he carried. The rain had subsided, leaving a sheen on the stones that mirrored the sun as it peeked through the parting clouds.

The docks teemed with life, the chaos of merchants and sailors going about their business, the cacophony of seagulls, ship crews, and merchants' voices intermingling to create a symphony of life along the river.

The scent of saltwater, fish, and exotic spices filled the air, fuelling Seth's determination as he navigated through the throngs of people. He scanned the faces around him in case she was running errands for her aunt. He searched for the familiar countenance that had haunted his dreams and filled his waking thoughts but there was no sign of her.

He rounded the corner at the end of the street and spotted the Jolly Jack ahead. Behind the grimy stone building, the river shimmered in the sunlight, reflecting the vibrant colours of the ships and the myriad of goods that passed through the port. He expected there would be sailors standing outside to enjoy an afternoon drink, but the front was empty. As he drew closer, he realised that the place was all shut up. He ducked under the low porch roof and put his shoulder into the door to open it, but it didn't budge.

"Go away!" Seth heard the muffled voice through the wood but tried the door again anyway. "We're closed!" Seth knocked twice more and listened to the muffled cursing emanating through the wood.

The bolts creaked and protested as they were pulled back, the complaining sound matching James' furious expression as his face emerged through the gap between the door and the frame.

"I said we're shut, you bleedin' – oh, it's you."

Seth smiled tentatively. "Good afternoon, Mr Tomlinson. Might Ella be home?"

The landlord held his faltering gaze for a moment before the door slammed shut. Seth frowned at the door, alarm racing across his nerve endings. This wasn't how he'd expected the day to go at all. He'd never known James Tomlinson to turn away trade so why would his business be closed up? He raised his hand to knock once more, ready to demand to know where the woman he loved was when James opened the door fully and gave a sharp jerk of his head. "Come on in."

Seth removed his hat and ducked his head as he stepped into the dimly lit room. The place was empty, save for Elsie and Maud, though he homed in on just one face – Ella's. Her eyes widened in surprise as she saw Seth. She offered him a tentative smile that buoyed his confidence though uncertainty flickered in her gaze. He was instantly soothed just by the sight of her. "Hello."

James shut the door behind him, sending the locks back home. "Sorry about the," his hand rolled in the air as if to encompass what had just transpired. "It's just, we've had some news."

It was then that Seth's avid gaze moved to the self-effacing man sitting next to Ella. His silver-brown hair was swept back from his shiny forehead, wire spectacles perching at the end of his thin nose. The brown suit lent a bookish air to him although Seth pegged him as a man of professional means by the assessing look that he was getting off him.

Ella's tongue wet her lips, a slight smile curving her mouth as she sat back. The table they sat at was covered with papers. "W-what are you doing here?"

Seth swallowed, apprehension fluttering in his throat now that the time had come for him to tell her his feelings. What if he was too late?

He took a step closer, his hands trembling as he tried to find the right words. "There's something I need to tell you," he began, his voice barely steady. "Something I should've said long ago." He glanced about the group, their expressions ranging from furious defiance to all-out amusement. "Can we speak in private?"

"Seth, I –"

Panic clutched at his heart, pushing through his fear and embarrassment when he realised that she was about to turn him away again. "Please, Ella. What you said to me yesterday outside the hotel – I love you, too. I'm a dullard for not telling you sooner. I want to tell you every day. I've told my father all about you, about how I am willing to give up the business if it means I can't live my life spending every day loving you."

Her brows shot up and she blinked at him. He pushed on, nonetheless.

"Ella, I love you. I've loved you for so long, and I couldn't bear the thought of losing you without telling you how I truly feel. I know the world is vast, and there are countless adventures to be had, but all I want is to share them with you."

His heart drummed and he was certain that they must all be able to hear its thrashing beat. He stared at her, searching for a glimmer of something, anything, to show him how she felt about his confession.

Ella pushed back from the table and rose to her feet. "You'd better take a seat. I have some news."

CHAPTER 38

lla

"I'M SORRY, Mr Harris, but there really must be some mistake," Ella said firmly. "My stepmother showed me the letters from my father's estate. The bank account was empty on account of a poor investment that my father had made years ago."

Mr Harris smiled as if he knew something that Ella didn't. He leaned back in his chair and thanked James for setting down a pint of ale and some slices of bread with cheese and dried beef. Mr Harris nudged back the plate so that he could lean his elbows on the table. James took up sentry leaning against the bar, arms folded and making no bones about the fact that he was listening in.

Mr Harris began, "I knew your father. He was a

splendid chap, with a wonderful sense of humour and a very astute business brain. It's what made him so good at what he did. He and my brother, William, studied together."

Harris paused to take a sip of his drink, savouring the taste on his tongue as he swallowed. His mannerisms reminded Ella a little of old Finney. "William moved to America around twenty years ago. As with all friends, when life took over, they didn't see each other very often. William was at your parents' wedding, and he was on your father's side at your mother's funeral."

The door was rattled again, as more sailors came looking for the afternoon tipple. She could hear the grumbling as they moved on to the next tavern. Inside, the silence stretched on.

Ella had no recollection of ever having met a William Harris. When she said as much to Mr Harris, he gave a little shrug. "After your mother died, your father became a bit of a recluse."

James harrumphed in agreement. Ella looked at her uncle. "Do you know the man he speaks of?"

"Your father had many friends, Ella. And he was much older than me. It's possible, but I didn't go to school as he did." He spread his hands to indicate the public house in which they sat.

Mr Harris continued, "When your father was in need, he reached out to William. You see, it appears that your father's marriage to Clara was in trouble quite early on. Clara is an ambitious woman, and your father knew that if the worst were to happen to him, your future and finances could be called into question."

The realisation that her father hadn't been happy in his marriage to Clara for a long time saddened her. She wondered if he'd ever really known much happiness in his life at all.

"Your father wrote to William seeking opportunities to invest," Mr Harris said.

Ella nodded. "I knew that he'd made heavy investments overseas. Clara told me that it was this investment that bankrupted him."

The knowing smile was back on Mr Harris' face. He took another swallow of his drink before he reached inside his leather case and removed a brown folder. He set it on the table between them, his fingertips tapping it lightly. "Your father was shrewd, Ella. He never made a bad investment. He just made it look that way."

An audible gasp escaped Ella's mouth. "He tricked everybody?"

Mr Harris shook his head. "Not everybody, just his greedy young wife."

Ella frowned. Mr Harris opened the folder a took out a sheath of papers. "My brother died two years ago. His passing was sudden. All his clients passed over to his partners, but your father's investment needed special consideration. Your father came to pay his respects, but he was alone. He'd disguised it to his wife as a business trip.

After the interment, we sat down to enjoy a brandy and a cigar – your father always had the most excellent cigars –" His finger tapped the air, drawing a smile from her. "We sat up chatting until the early hours. He explained the arrangement he'd had with William, who'd been looking after his finances in secret, and I confirmed that the investments were safe.

But your father admitted to me that he was worried. He'd overheard his wife speaking unkindly to you. They had the most dreadful argument. The investment he'd made was doing considerably well. We decided that it would be best to hide it."

"Can you do that?"

Mr Harris nodded at James' question. "Using the right language and knowing the right people, yes. It was all above board legally. We paid the taxes due. It was just...hidden."

Ella blinked, trepidation rippling through her. "Hidden where?"

"Abroad. In a trust, until you came of age. And then it would be all yours."

Her mouth dropped open. "B-but I am of age."

Mr Harris grinned at her, eyes sparkling. "Exactly."

James elbowed his way off the bar. "Wait just a minute. All this time you've been looking for her to give her an inheritance?"

George Harris' brows rounded. "That's right. It only required a signature. We usually let our agents handle such tasks."

"He didn't look like a solicitor," Elsie said.

"We like to use ex-servicemen. They're usually grateful for the work and they tend to follow orders to the letter, which helps when you're dealing with the law." He took out a sheaf of papers, tapping the edges against the table. He arranged the ink well and the pen as he spoke, "Of course, had I known that your step-mother had caused such a commotion, I would have caught an earlier boat."

"Boat?" James asked.

"I joined William's practice in America. Before he died, he ensured that I knew what to do with this case. I suppose I should have been here as soon as you came of age, but time passes by quickly. It took a few weeks before the news of your father's death reached the other side of the Atlantic. A few more to get everything organised, as is the way of international law. I'm so very sorry to hear of his passing," Mr Harris' voice softened with compassion and Ella could only nod wordlessly as her throat squeezed with emotion. "William mentioned that his health fluctuated."

"She thinks Clara poisoned him the same way that she offed this latest one," Maud supplied.

Mr Harris' mouth compressed. "Well, that is grave news indeed. Perhaps William was right, after all."

"In what way?" Ella leaned forward.

"William hinted that your father had joked once or twice that he believed that he'd wake up with a knife in his neck. But they do say that poison is a woman's weapon."

Ella sighed softly. It didn't help her feelings of misery knowing that her father held his suspicions about what Clara was capable of. He could have divorced her, though he wouldn't have done that to Thomas. Henry Tomlinson was honourable right to the end.

"So, what exactly did Papa invest in?"

"A copper mine," Mr Harris leaned forward. "And the railway industry in America, amongst other things."

There was a beat of stunned silence.

"Yes, Miss Tomlinson. A considerable sum of money is yours." He flipped back the lid of the ink well. The door knocked again. James growled. "Go away!" But this time, the sailors weren't giving up so easily. They knocked again, despite her uncle bellowing, "We're closed!"

Her mind was trying to concentrate on what Mr Harris was indicating to her on the papers when she heard how her uncle's angry outburst altered down to a begrudging tone in the doorway. When she looked up at the man who'd stepped into the interior, her thoughts scattered to the wind like dandelion seeds in flight.

"Hello."

Seth. Her heart knocked against her ribcage but her overriding emotion was simply joyfulness. Joy at seeing him standing there when she'd been given such tremendous news. She tried to gather her erratic thoughts and asked him what he was doing there. He was nervous, she realised. From the way his eyes moved around the room, taking in her aunt's stern stare and glowering uncle, to Elsie's glee.

"Can we speak in private?"

She wanted to hear what he had to say. Of course, she did, but she needed to get what Mr Harris was saying to her straight in her mind. It sounded to her like Henry's business mind had protected her still. She couldn't be cross over the poor timing of Mr Harris' visit. Had he arrived sooner, she would never have reunited with her aunt and uncle. She wouldn't have known Finney, nor would she have become a fiddle player. She never would have known that Seth Milford nor would she have fallen for him.

As his words tumbled over the other like a torrent of water after breaking the dam, her heart filled with love.

He loves me, too.

"Please, Seth, you'd better take a seat. I have some news." She owed it to him to be upfront. This news changed everything. Confusion clouded Seth's eyes. "This is Mr George Harris," She pressed her fingertips to her chin and frowned at the solicitor. "I'm sorry, what with everything you've said this afternoon, I've forgotten what company you said you were from."

George Harris was unfazed by the interruption. He partly rose in his seat and extended a hand to Seth, assessing the newcomer with open amusement. "Clancy, Burke, and Harris in Boston."

Seth's dark gaze flicked to Ella's and back as he shook the man's hand and then slowly lowered himself into a seat. "You're a long way from home, Mr Harris."

The solicitor chuckled as he resumed his seat. "Well, this young lady has proven to be more than tricky to track down, but I wouldn't have made the trip if not for a promise I made to her father."

"This is Seth Milford," she indicated to Mr Harris. "He owns a shipping company."

"Milford Shipping?" George asked.

"That's right."

The solicitor nodded, laughter shining in his eyes as Seth began to fidget. "I know of it. A fine company. Your grandfather was a force to be reckoned with."

A smile slid briefly over Seth's lips. He was waiting for a further explanation until Ella realised that Mr Harris wouldn't divulge anything further without her permission.

"My father and William, Mr Harris' brother, were close friends," she clarified. "Papa sought out William's advice on where to invest in America, where he lived. Like my father, William was a commercial solicitor with wealthy clients, and Papa trusted his judgement."

With her implicit approval for Seth to be included in the discussion, Mr Harris continued the conversation. Ella observed Seth's expression as the solicitor described her father's efforts to provide for his children while keeping the fortune hidden from Clara. She couldn't help but wonder if Seth would find this information off-putting.

She had always known Henry Tomlinson as a kind and compassionate man, but concealing a fortune from his widow could be perceived as cold and calculating. Seth's face remained expressionless, his gaze shifting between the legal documents and the solicitor. She remembered that she'd teased him about his card game face and wished for even a glimmer of what he was thinking. If he glanced at her, it was brief and fleeting, and her concern grew that this revelation might not be what he had hoped for. Her newfound wealth would undoubtedly alter their relationship dynamic. Now, Thomas could remain in school, and her aunt and uncle could hire help, as she would likely need her uncle's assistance in managing the business.

"Who has been managing the assets up until now?" Seth inquired.

The solicitor seemed pleased by Seth's question and pulled out additional papers, explaining that Henry had appointed William, and subsequently George, as care-takers. The investment had proven to be secure and had experienced consistent growth.

Her body went rigid with tension when Seth looked up from the papers. His gaze searched her face.

"Your father was a smart man," he said to her, admiration edging his voice. "He concealed the investment cleverly. The language he used ensures protection for both you and Thomas, so no one else can claim it. However, I'm not clear about one thing. You mentioned that Thomas wasn't your blood relative."

"I don't know if Papa ever knew the truth," Ella said quietly. "Nobody did. I only guessed once Thomas was standing alongside Dr Seward. Papa was often away working after marrying Clara. Dr Seward looked after my father's health, but he was Clara's constant companion."

"He knew."

Ella whirled to stare at George Harris. "H-he did?"

"As I said, he was a brilliant man. He'd returned from a long trip away to news that Clara was expecting. She claimed to be further along than she was. Dr Seward looked after her pregnancy and your father grew suspicious of their relationship, though he never dared to ask his wife outright. But he knew that Thomas wasn't his child. It was what compelled him to protect you and seek out William's advice years later when he realised that his wife wasn't at all grateful that he'd done the honourable thing.

Still, Henry would never cast an innocent out. It seems that Henry knew that Seward was an adulterer. Dare I say that his philandering ways caught up with him in the end."

Ella rubbed her hand shakily across her lips. No, her father wouldn't take out his hurt on Thomas. But he would make sure that Clara didn't get what she was after. She didn't trust her voice to say anything more.

"Secreting the funds indicates he didn't trust his wife not to do precisely what she has done."

Ella felt relieved when she realised that Seth understood her father's intentions, and her shoulders relaxed slightly. "That's exactly right," she whispered thickly.

Seth smiled at her, making her heart race. He then addressed George, "What are your obligations regarding the investment once ownership is transferred?"

"That would be up to the new owner," George

replied cautiously. "But if you're asking whether Miss Tomlinson will continue to receive the same level of care and support her father did," the solicitor gave Seth a steady look that hinted at his astuteness, "Henry Tomlinson was my friend too. If Ella's suspicions about his death are correct, then my friend was murdered. I'll do everything in my power to advise her and ensure the funds are used properly."

Seth seemed content with this response. "That's good. She'll need guidance until she learns what to do."

A joyful smile spread across her face. It appeared that Seth expected her to take an active role in managing the business, an idea she hadn't considered before.

Seth's dark eyes focused on her. She wanted to reach out to him but clenched her fists under the table instead.

"I'm truly happy for you, Ella."

Maud let out a bitter laugh. "You're only saying that because she's now sitting on a fortune."

Seth turned, his brows furrowing. "I beg your pardon?"

"Your father will approve of her now that she's rich, won't he?"

"Aunt Maud," Ella interjected, noticing the self-reproach on Seth's face. "Please, let's not be unkind to each other. Seth came here without knowing the truth – how could he know when we've just found out ourselves?" She looked at Seth, disbelief filling her.

"Did you really tell your father about me?" she asked, her stomach fluttering.

He nodded. "I did. I gave up my claim to the company."

"I wouldn't want to come between you and your family though, not when I know how much they mean to you."

He offered a half-smile and a self-conscious shrug. "Turns out, my father needs me more than he'd like to admit. He's agreed to the changes I proposed."

"That's fantastic news."

"I made my intentions towards you perfectly clear with him. I am to extend an invitation to both you and to your aunt and uncle so that my parents might meet your family."

"Golly," Ella breathed. "I can't quite believe it."

"What will you do now?" Her uncle's soft question interrupted her intense gaze with Seth.

Ella turned to face her uncle, who appeared desolate. "Papa has ensured that we all benefit from this. Thomas can stay in school. I can even hire someone to contest Dr Seward's estate now."

Her uncle's smile didn't completely erase the sadness in his eyes. "I'm happy for you, Ella. But I'll miss you."

Ella approached him and stopped in front of him. "It sounds like you think I'll leave you all without a second thought. That's not going to happen."

James shrugged. "You have money now, and it seems you have a husband-to-be."

She placed a hand on his arm. "I need my family, Uncle. You both have business experience, and I am going to need all the help I can get. I wouldn't turn my back on either of you. Papa was right – coming here was the best thing for me. You saved me, gave me a purpose." James' eyes turned misty, and he opened his arms to her. She stepped into the embrace and sighed happily. "Besides, who else will play the fiddle for you? I am the Dockyard Darling, after all."

lla

"Mr Grimley," Ella stared at the schoolmaster. His dark-brown suit looked as out of place as a fish on the riverbank amongst the sea of sailors in their oiled canvas trousers and smocks that filled the Jolly Jack.

James had opened the doors for the evening trade. He was currently sitting in the far corner with Seth and George Harris, each with a smile on their face and a pint of ale in front of them. Her heart swelled with warmth, knowing Seth was hers, though they had not found a private moment to speak. Seth had asked to speak to James briefly. She needn't have worried though as they returned shortly after and invited Mr Harris to join them for supper. Maud had gone for a lie-down, leaving Elsie and Ella to feed and water the customers.

Mr Grimley navigated his way to the front of the bar, and his grave expression sent a shiver of apprehension through Ella. With her nerves already frayed from the day's events, she dreaded any further news. "Can we talk somewhere?" he asked.

Ella's smile faltered and she nodded. She set the glasses down on the bar top and held up her fingers to Elsie that she needed five minutes. Elsie's head bobbed in acknowledgement, her gaze sliding over to Seth and her uncle. Seth must have spotted the teacher because he was sliding out from the bench and heading her way without her needing to signal to him.

She followed the teacher out through the front door, stopping short when she spotted Milly and an unfamiliar, stern-faced man.

"Milly," Ella rushed to embrace her friend, her mind reeling with all she had to share. But as she hugged Milly, she noticed her friend's eyes were fixed on Mr Grimley. Ella couldn't help but wonder if there was more to Milly's presence than merely guiding the teacher to the public house.

"Hello, miss," Milly replied, and as they stepped apart, Ella caught a fleeting, meaningful glance exchanged between her friend and the schoolmaster. Her attention was diverted by the tall, intimidating stranger.

"This is Mr Reginald Andrews," Mr Grimley introduced the man. "He's with the police."

A chilling dread enveloped Ella, and she wrapped her arms around herself for comfort.

"Ella? What is it?" Seth's voice carried unease as he joined them, his gaze fixed on Mr Grimley.

Intent on allaying any concerns he harboured toward the teacher; she made brief introductions.

"Remember you asked me to try and find someone who could help Thomas?" Mr Grimley didn't waste any time getting to the point.

"That was only yesterday," she said.

"Dr Seward was a popular man, even if his morals weren't as clean as a whistle," Mr Grimley said. "Many people wanted to help him. All of them were shocked to the core over his death. One of our parents is a barrister, who was able to pull some strings."

"You believe your father was murdered?" Reginald Andrews enquired, his words brisk and abrupt.

"T-that's right," Ella stammered softly, grateful when Seth draped his coat over her shoulders.

"What's this all about?" Seth aligned himself alongside her, offering silent support.

Reginald appraised Seth with a hawkish gaze, but Seth remained unshaken. "We were searching Mr Seward's townhouse, where a woman by the name of Mary Smith resided." *The mistress.* Ella wondered about the woman, but the policeman continued, "She was having some difficulty gaining access to the doctor's legal documents, but she knew that there were funds that were supposed to be allocated to her. With the help of the barrister that Grimley connected us to, she was able to access those documents rather quickly, as it goes."

He looked at Ella, his gaze unapologetic. "Dr Seward had left a letter for his son. It acknowledges the child as his, plus one other child – a younger daughter."

Ella's exhaled her relief in a gust. "That's good news for Thomas, at least. Is he alright?"

"The young man is at school. As yet, we haven't revealed the content of the letter to him," Reginald said.

Ella furrowed her brow. "He should know. He was worried about his schooling."

Mr Grimley's mouth flattened into a line. "There's more, Ella."

Ella's eyes searched the group, silently urging them to continue.

"The letter was a confession," Mr Andrews divulged. "In the event of his sudden and unexplained death, Dr Seward wanted it to be known that he played a part in the poisoning of and resulting death of a Mr Henry Tomlinson."

CHAPTER 40

he sun dipped low in the sky, painting the scene in hues of gold and crimson as the final rays caressed the docklands horizon. The water lapped gently against the wooden piers, sparkling in the embers of the sun.

The day's bustle had begun to subside, making way for the calm embrace of twilight. The scent of saltwater mingled with the fragrance of nearby fish markets, a potent reminder of the symbiotic relationship between the city and its maritime lifeblood. Tall masts of docked ships stood as silent sentinels, their sails furled and flags fluttering lightly in the evening breeze.

Ella stood on the quayside, her eyes tracing the intricate lattice of ropes and rigging that adorned the ships like delicate webs. The day, much like the past few weeks, had been one revelation after another, with visits to the police investigating the Seward murder.

The police seemed delighted to be able to add her

words to the weight of the evidence that stacked up against Clara. Milly and her Mr Grimley had eaten at the Jolly Jack before they'd caught the train back. It made her smile that her friend had found managed to find work nearby the school where Mr Grimley worked, though she would guess that her friend wouldn't be in employment for much longer once Mr Grimley proposed. She did have half a mind that Milly would come and work for her one day, but it seemed her friend had higher ambitions than remaining a housemaid all her days.

She sought solace in the dying embers of the day. The ships and the sunset eased the turmoil in her mind. The dry smell of the burlap tickled her nose and old Finney's toothless grin shimmered at the edges of her memory. She knew that her father would have liked the man. Thinking about her father squeezed her heart painfully. If only he'd divorced Clara, perhaps he'd still be alive, as would Dr Seward.

Seth was right. She couldn't keep going round and round with speculation on what might have been. Her future had been secured by her father. Thomas would be able to stay in school. She would write to him and let him know that she would always be his sister. She had to focus on her future. She needed to learn about business and how to engage with the trades across the Atlantic. She'd already started. Her uncle would be entrenched fully. She had made James a promise to secure the Jolly Jack, and they'd joked about another public house being named after her father. The draught danced through her hair, causing it to fan out behind her like a dark, silken curtain.

Seth, standing close by, observed the play of emotions on Ella's face as she took in the view. The scene before them was a testament to the industriousness of the age, the resilience of the human spirit, and the eternal dance between nature and human endeavour. Yet he couldn't take his eyes off her.

"It's breath-taking, isn't it?" Ella murmured, her voice barely audible above the distant cries of seagulls and the soft creaking of moored vessels. "I stand here and marvel at everything man has achieved. The mix of old and new ways... makes me feel both humbled and invigorated, like a reminder that we are part of something much bigger than we can ever comprehend."

The setting sun cast long shadows across the cobblestones, and the gas lamps flickered to life, their warm glow winking to life along the river's edge.

"I only have eyes for you tonight," Seth reached for her hand, his fingers intertwining with hers. Awareness zinged through her blood and her breath caught in her throat as she turned to him, her eyes shining with unspoken emotion. "You're captivating, Ella. The generosity of your spirit knows no bounds. Your actions have secured not only the future of your aunt and uncle, and your stepbrother, but also that of Elsie and Milly."

"Do you think me foolish and irresponsible?"

Seth shook his head. "Far from it."

"The money is more than I will need in my lifetime."

"And our children's," Seth added.

"Perhaps," she ventured softly, "it's moments like these that remind us why we endure the hardships of life – so that we can share in the beauty of the world with those we care for."

Seth's lips curled into a tender smile, his eyes reflecting the colours of the dying sun. "You always have a way of finding the light in the darkness, Ella," he said, his voice carrying the warmth of genuine admiration. "It's just another reason why I love you."

Her eyes drifted closed, a smile playing across her lips. "Say that again."

Seth lifted both hands to his lips, brushing his mouth across her knuckles. "I love you, Ella."

Her eyes opened, and she could see the sentiment mirror that coursed through her mirrored in his gaze.

"I meant everything I said the other day. I want a life with you."

"Even if I don't know quite how that will look right now? There is bound to be fallout with Clara."

"I promise to stand at your side," he said, "through thick and thin."

"Your family will undoubtedly be caught up in the scandal."

"Hush," Seth whispered, closing the gap between them. His breath fanned along her skin as his cheek grazed her ear. "Please, don't fret about this. I will prepare them. I will help you uncover the truth about your father. We won't rest until we have justice for him."

Her skin tautened with goosebumps as the significance of his words sank in. She leaned back, her eyes shimmering as her heart swelled with gratitude and affection. She could sense the depth of his thoughts. Uncle James had been as absorbed in the complexities of the paperwork and business tasks as Seth had ever since Mr Harris had left. Ella knew that she would rely heavily on them both in navigating the intricate waters of trade and society. Her father had gifted her a tremendous future.

Yet, at this moment, as they stood together on the quayside, all their challenges and uncertainties seemed to fade into the background, leaving only the wonder of each other.

"I'm grateful to have you here by my side."

"I want to marry you, Ella. I want to be your husband and have the world know that I love you. I have already sought permission from your uncle."

She blinked at him. "Is that why you went upstairs with him the day that Mr Harris arrived?"

Seth's mouth hooked up on one side, and a dimple winked in his cheek. "I think he was touched that I did so, but I want this to be done properly."

"Sarah Milford raised a gentleman," she murmured.

"I'm not sure she'd always agree with that statement," he chuckled lightly.

"What if they don't like me?" She asked. "Your family, I mean."

"Then it will be their loss, my love."

"What about my fiddle playing?"

"Ella," Seth said, cupping her face in his hands. "Please, stop worrying. We will work it all out – together. We have a lifetime to answer those questions. Can I kiss you now?"

She grinned up at him and nodded. Her eyes drifted closed as his head lowered to hers, covering her mouth in a gentle kiss. She sighed softly, supplicant under his touch, as she surrendered herself to his love.

As the sun dipped below the horizon, Ella and Seth stood in the deepening blue as twilight cloaked the docklands. She rested her head on his shoulder and he held her close to him, content to look out across the shimmering river, the gaslights dancing across the rippling surface. Ella knew that although the world around them might change, their connection would remain steadfast – a beacon of her hope in the ever-changing tides of life.

EPILOGUE

The Jolly Jack was abuzz with life as Ella's strings danced along to a spirited tune, prompting the crowd to clap and skip in time with the music.

Her feet tapped to the rhythm, and she exchanged a joyful glance with Archie, who accompanied her on the piano. His fingers flew across the keys while her bow gracefully kept pace.

Scanning the sea of jubilant faces, Ella realized how much she had missed this. She caught sight of her husband seated next to Thomas at the edge of the dance floor. Thomas, laughing and clapping along with his brother-in-law, had followed Henry's wishes by pursuing a career in law, guided by Philip and Giles, Seth's young, fun-loving brother. Ella was confident that Thomas would achieve the success he had always dreamed of, thanks to his diligent studies.

Philip had become a beacon of support in Thomas'

life, offering the stability the young man craved. Impressed by Thomas from the outset, it was Philip's unwavering advocacy to Home Secretary Henry Matthews that had resulted in Clara's sentence after her guilty verdict being reduced from the death penalty to twenty years imprisonment. Despite the evidence overwhelmingly supporting Clara, the judge acknowledged that Dr Seward's letter could have been written out of malice. Clara's strong denial of the allegations was enough to convince the judge to spare her life.

In some ways, Ella was relieved. Thomas had already lost both Henry and Dr Seward, and he deserved no further heartache. However, he refused to visit his mother, leaving Clara to spend her remaining days alone in her cell. For a woman as vain as Clara, Ella knew that this isolation would be a fate worse than the gallows.

James' northern factory thrived, providing materials for Seth's ships. Under George Harris' supervision, the mine had been sold, and the profits were invested in both English railways and American ventures in the West. The combined forces of James, Seth, and Philip formed an impressive alliance.

Milly Grimley and her husband occupied the table next to Ella's aunt and uncle. Having recently secured a position at a country school, the schoolmaster would now see his wife more often. Milly had played a crucial role in convincing Cook to come and work for Ella, and in return, Ella had offered Cook a generous wage and ample support via a thriving kitchen team in her autumn years.

Ella's greatest joy, young Henry, sat upon Maud's lap, his chubby hands moving in time with the music. Although young Henry adored his grandmother, Sarah, the bond between the small boy and his great-aunt was truly special.

Across the room, Elsie served drinks, delighted by the additional business that the return of the dockyard darling had brought to the Jolly Jack. James had no regrets about appointing Elsie as landlady, as the move to the countryside had improved Maud's health and brought them closer to Ella and Seth's home.

As Ella slowed the music to a tender, soaring melody, she pondered what Philip and Sarah would think of the Jolly Jack. They had seen her perform in London's music halls, but Sarah had never ventured to the docklands.

Ella knew that her in-laws couldn't comprehend her insistence on playing at such venues when she no longer needed the income. She was no longer merely the dockyard darling; she had become the city's darling, drawing crowds from far and wide. When Sarah expressed her confusion, Ella would simply smile and say that the dockyard would forever hold a piece of her heart.

It was here that she had found herself. Where she'd discovered family, a home, her friends. Her eyes met her husband's richly dark gaze through the hazy smoke that lingered near the low ceiling. Even now, her pulse skidded as their eyes locked. She brought the song to an end, to rapturous applause and calls for more but she carefully placed Finney's fiddle back in its case, with a smile.

It was here that she'd met her love. The man who'd allowed her to live her truth. The one who'd kept his promise and stood at her side, even as the scandal of Clara had raged throughout the land. Although, she knew that her days of playing must be put off for a while. Tonight, when they were alone and in bed, she would tell her husband that she was expecting their second child.

Another link to their lives. A life that had begun right here in the heart of this old city.

ABOUT THE AUTHOR

Annie Shields lives in Shropshire with her husband and two daughters. When she doesn't have her nose in a book, you'll find her exploring old buildings and following historical trails, dragging her ever-patient husband along with his map.

She combines her love of the Victorian Era with fiction, sprinkling some real-life facts throughout the romance stories.

If you would like to be amongst the first to hear when she releases a new book and free books by similar authors, you can join her mailing list HERE

As a thank you, you will receive a FREE copy of her eBook Tilly's Story - the prequel to her popular series The Slum Sisters

Your details won't be passed along to anyone else and you can unsubscribe at any time.

ALSO BY ANNIE SHIELDS

The Queen of Thieves

Trixie White must learn to survive on the streets of Victorian London by all means necessary. But, working in a team of pickpockets, her quick hands and courage make her stand out. But when the Queen of Thieves is made to choose between the man that she loves or protecting her little sister, Trixie's battle takes a dangerous turn.

The Swindler's Daughter

After she discovers that her wealthy family are rotten to the core, Mollie Webster is cast out onto the streets of London. Frightened and alone, she must learn to trust her instincts in order to survive. But when Jack Taylor is thrust back into her life, can she truly believe that the only man she's ever loved isn't another thug sent by her family to destroy her?

The Tale of a Christmas Foundling

Ivy & Rose have very different lives. One is brought up in the city orphanage after being abandoned at birth; the other grows up in a house of wealth and privilege. But wealth doesn't always equal happiness. Follow this tale to find out how these two women are inextricably linked by a dark secret that will change their lives forever.

Printed in Great Britain
by Amazon

26829584R00175